## Prais

# YUMA

"The unlikely search for a buried Spanish galleon in the Yuma desert propels the action in Steven Law's *Yuma Gold*. The possibility of buried treasure brings forth plot twists, action, and a cast of characters you won't soon forget."

—Thomas Cobb, author of *Crazy Heart*

"Start reading at your own risk. You won't want to put it down. Memorable characters, a captivating setting, and exciting plot twists will keep you turning the pages."

—Cotton Smith, author of *Ride for Rule Cordell*

## SALVATION

"What the hell!" Mulcov shouted.

The Russian just stood there glaring, his oily body glistening under the lamplight. He held out his arms as if protecting the women.

"I am here to free them," Enrique said. "*Mujeres*, you are free to go as you please."

"Like hell," Mulcov said. "Who the hell do you think you are?" By this time he was growling, arms arched at his sides like a hairless grizzly bear. He charged Enrique and tackled him to the ground. The weight of the man on top of him made it difficult for him to breathe, and Enrique could not move him. It got worse when Mulcov brought a forearm up and laid it over his throat and pushed down with all his weight. Enrique could feel the blood compressing his skull, and his very life vanishing before him.

Pang jumped in on top of Mulcov, but not even the swift moves of martial arts could penetrate the stout layers of this bear of a man. A sudden noise made everything stop. Mulcov stopped growling and his arm slowly lifted off Enrique's neck. Enrique gasped and choked. Pang backed away. Mulcov rose slowly with a barrel of a gun pressed firmly against his head . . .

*Berkley titles by Steven Law*

EL PASO WAY
YUMA GOLD

# EL PASO
## ★ WAY ★

### BLOOD FOR JUSTICE

## STEVEN LAW

**B**

BERKLEY BOOKS, NEW YORK

**THE BERKLEY PUBLISHING GROUP**
Published by the Penguin Group
Penguin Group (USA)
375 Hudson Street, New York, New York 10014, USA

USA | Canada | UK | Ireland | Australia | New Zealand | India | South Africa | China

Penguin Books Ltd., Registered Offices: 80 Strand, London WC2R 0RL, England
For more information about the Penguin Group, visit penguin.com.

EL PASO WAY

A Berkley Book / published by arrangement with the author

*El Paso Way* is based on a short story of the same title, which was originally published by
Amazon Shorts.

Berkley Books are published by The Berkley Publishing Group.
BERKLEY® is a registered trademark of Penguin Group (USA).
The "B" design is a trademark of Penguin Group (USA).

For information, address: The Berkley Publishing Group,
a division of Penguin Group (USA),
375 Hudson Street, New York, New York 10014.

ISBN: 978-0-425-26152-1

PUBLISHING HISTORY
Berkley mass-market edition / October 2013

PRINTED IN THE UNITED STATES OF AMERICA

10  9  8  7  6  5  4  3  2  1

Cover illustration by Dennis Lyall.
Cover design by Diana Kolsky.
Interior text design by Kelly Lipovich.

*Dedicated to, and in memory of,* mis abuelos:
*Virgil Andrew Anderson and Victor Neal Crawford*

*Sí.* El Paso was the answer—not a good one, but the best under the circumstances; perhaps the only one.
—Norman Zollinger, *Not of War Only*


Notions of chance and fate are the preoccupation of men engaged in rash undertakings.
—Cormac McCarthy, *Blood Meridian*

# ENRIQUE OSORIO

## SPRING 1876
### North of Tumacacori Mission, Arizona Territory

Enrique Osorio lay on his stomach, gripping with an eager hand the end of a willow blade snare. If not for the patience encouraged by his grandfather, he would likely have pulled too quickly, missing the jackrabbit's hind leg and sending it scurrying off into the Sonora wild. But Enrique was a good student, and he'd learned that the rewards of the hunter were the motivation needed to succeed. Like how pleased his mother would be when he returned with the meat for supper. The pride his father would have noticing his own eleven-year-old son approaching manhood and being able help provide for his family. His sister Amelia's love of taking the stew meat and wrapping it in a tortilla with squash and *frijoles*. They were fine rewards, but premature thoughts that went against the wise teachings of his grandfather. "Hunt first, rejoice later," the old man would have said.

The jackrabbit foraged on the tufts of grasses sprouting through the sand, but Enrique set his snare loop near a cluster of barrel cactus, thinking that the hare might be thirsty and, like other rodents of the desert, draw water from the plants' flesh. The animal made a few short hops toward the cactus, and the boy was feeling more confident in his decision, but a nearby scream made the jackrabbit stop and rise up on its hind legs. The cry came again, an eerie echo that caused the rabbit to run for safety.

Disappointed, Enrique rose to his bare feet, coiled the snare, and tucked it under the plaited leather belt that fit tight around his white pima shirt and trousers. He found the direction of the sound, which had worn to intermittent moans and grunts. His first thought was a coydog fight. Then he visualized a mountain lion down from the Sierrita Mountains ambushing a pronghorn in the arroyo. No, he decided it was neither. It was like no animal he had ever heard before, but whatever it was, the predator had most certainly won over its prey.

He walked closer to the strange noises, hoping to catch a glimpse of something new. They came from an area beyond a stand of saguaros and ocotillos and down in an arroyo where he couldn't see the cause. He treaded slow and leery down a deer trail toward the crying and grunting, and stepped quickly backward when he caught an odd motion out of the corner of his eye. The feeling was queer and foreign, as if this place that had been his lifelong home was suddenly trying to fool him. Scared, he hunched to his knees, leaned down on his hands, and peered back to see what this strange moment would reveal.

Indeed it was an odd sight, and not crazed animals as he had thought, but a big, hairy man pulling up his trousers. His hair was long like the Apache but this man was not Apache. Though tanned, his flesh was thick and his hair curly like that of a gringo and not likely a Mexican. Enrique could not comprehend where such a man would have come from or, more interesting, what he was doing.

The boy backed around and off the trail and walked through the saguaros until he could peek through and see the face of the man, and now he saw more than one person; he also saw a much smaller person, a teenage girl. The man led her by a rope tied around her neck, and her hands were tied together, her dress was badly soiled and torn, and her long brown hair was in disarray. When she turned sideways, Enrique could see that there was a strip of red cloth tied between her lips and around to the back of her head. Her face was youthful and somewhat familiar, as was her dress. She cried and moaned, and the man jerked the rope harder.

Enrique understood none of this.

Not until she fell down, and the man jerked her up to where Enrique could see her in full frontal view, did he recognize his elder and only sibling, Amelia. Fear swept through Enrique like a blast from a furnace, and he knew that she was in dire trouble. He wished he could help her but was also certain that there was nothing an eleven-year-old boy and a willow snare could do to stop such a big man. He would have to go get his father. Though his father was a quiet man, he was stern and stout, and definitely one who could set this man straight.

* * *

Enrique ran the trail back to his home with a different kind of anticipation than he had hoped, but he no longer cared about the rewards of a hunter. The look on Amelia's face was all he could see, and it generated a higher energy to get to his father before his sister was hurt any more. He wondered if the man would kill her, but he quickly realized that such thoughts wouldn't get him home any faster.

The only thing that slowed him was the sudden sight of black smoke billowing near their adobe. When he arrived, he saw that it was the adobe itself that made the smoke. Thick, curling columns rolled out the doorway and from under the lean-to where his mother cooked their meals. Their goats lay scattered and slaughtered in their own blood and excrement. Chickens lay dead; others ran about, and their detached feathers whipped in the breeze and through the black plumes. He heard the brays of the burros then saw a strange man gathering them and pulling them with leather leads. Unlike the man he'd seen with Amelia, this man was definitely Apache, with long, straight black hair, a deerskin cap, a loincloth, and leggings. He didn't wear a shirt, and the bronze tone of his lean, muscular chest and stomach stood out against the tawny desert backdrop.

Enrique crept around to the back of the adobe, where his father and grandfather had built a corral for their stock. Several of the fence rails were loose and had been knocked down, and the goats and burros were all gone. Someone lay facedown inside the corral, and as he ran to that person, Enrique recognized the homespun clothes of his father, now all soiled and soaked with blood. He knelt beside the body and turned it over to find a bloody, gaping wound on his father's forehead and his eyes open but lifeless, peering off into nothing.

Enrique's eyes welled with tears. *"Papá?"*

The Apache called out loudly, and a frightened Enrique ran toward the smoldering adobe and fell to his hands and knees. Heat radiated through the wall and he was afraid to touch it, but it was the only thing protecting him from the sight of the Apache, so he remained behind it. He peeked around the corner and now saw two men, and though the second man also looked Apache, he was dressed in a gringo's hat and long blue coat. The tips of his shoes were strange, in that they shined and reflected the sunlight as if they were polished like a wide knife blade. He carried two dead chickens by their feet, and a basket of dried fruits that his mother had made for his father for a hunting trip into the mountains. The boy could not understand who these men were and why they were doing this to his family and home.

Afraid that the men might see him, he crawled to the lean-to and came upon his mother drooped over the furnace where she cooked their meals. He turned her and became overwhelmed by a choking stench of burned flesh. He called out to her then laid his head on her chest, embraced her, and wept. Both his parents dead. It couldn't be.

The Apache tongue of the two men grew louder, and the boy raised his head as they walked toward the lean-to. The one carrying the chickens saw him and shouted, and the other ran toward him. Never had he been so fearful for his own life, and though he had been feeling the desire to be dead like his parents, his instincts told him he should run.

He grabbed a machete that lay near his mother's hand

and ran toward the burro stable that stood on the far side of the battered corral, opposite the adobe, and was the only structure that was not burning or beat down. When inside, he ducked down and tried to hide in the darkness of a corner. Save for the braying of the burros outside and the crackling of the adobe fire, he heard nothing but his own deep breaths and rapid heartbeat.

He sat there for only a short moment before footsteps outside the stable assured him that he would be found. He remembered a day when he was looking for a lost milk goat and found a doe in the stable. His coming upon her frightened her, and though his eyes would usually adjust to the darkness, she milled and stirred to where the dust inside the stable was so thick he couldn't see anything, and the goat ran right by him.

Enrique dragged the machete sporadically across the floor of dry soil and muck until a dusty haze formed over the light that came in from the doorway. He tried not to cough and held his arm over his nose and mouth so he wouldn't inhale the mess into his lungs. He squinted over his arm and backed next to the doorway, and when the man leaned inside, Enrique slung the machete into him. The boy dropped the weapon and ran out, and looked back only for a moment, to see the Apache lying on the ground, wide-eyed and screaming, with blood spurting from his neck and onto his face and chest. Though Enrique knew he had needed to kill the man, it stunned and horrified him to see what he had done.

The other man dropped the chickens and basket, drew a knife, and came running. Enrique ran behind the stable and into the wilderness. Whether the man was close behind him or not, he couldn't tell, but for all he knew he could feel the Apache's hot breath on his back, so he just kept running. He came upon a cliff and hid behind the largest of the rocks in the talus. Gasping, he curled up with his knees against his chest. He tried to muffle the sounds of his breathing in the bend of his arm. Then he heard the man, whose feet beat the ground in a running stride, which slowed as he came near. Enrique could not plan a way out of this one. He thought of picking up a rock and hitting the man in the head, but before the decision had been made, the man turned and ran down a trail into the desert.

The boy could not believe the man had missed him, as the Apache were excellent trackers and more savvy in the wilderness than any *Criollo*. But this *was* no ordinary Apache. He wore gringo's clothes and strange shoes. Maybe he was an outcast from his clan, left to fend for himself in his own ways. The boy could not be sure, but he was grateful for his luck and for the chance for his heart to calm.

He remained hid in the rocks for several hours. The entire episode kept replaying in his mind—the strangeness of the men, their voices, their clothes, the looks on his parents' faces, Amelia's eyes when they opened, the sweat, the smoke, the blood. It was all too overwhelming for the young hunter, and since he was not sure it was good to be alive, all he could do was weep.

# PANG LO

Pang Lo looked forward to quiet evenings with his family—content moments, with the toned down noises of a city at rest outside their tent and the fragrance of incense to liven the dry desert air. He sat on a pillow in front of a short square table and bowed to Hingon, his father, whose years of enlightenment were evident in his calmness, as well as the few thin gray hairs that hung from his chin and on each side of his mouth. And Pang was proud of the women in his family: his sister, Mun Lo, and his fiancée, Sai Min. They approached the table dressed in red-and-black batik robes, their hair pinned up neatly in large black buns and their faces the color of fresh snow. They served soup and rice in white ceramic bowls, and tea in matching cups, and then bowed to the men.

The young women sat down on their pillows across from the men and waited for them to sample the food. Pang pinched a knot of rice with his chopsticks and dipped it into the soup. He was sure that it would be good. Mun was an excellent cook, taught by his mother. Pang was about to savor the rice on his tongue, when the flap of the canvas tent flew open and he dropped the rice into his lap. He jumped from his pillow and Hingon grabbed his arm.

Three men, with darkness behind them and amber lamplight on their swarthy faces, walked slowly toward the table. The two in the lead wore serapes and straw sombreros. The last of them wore black—all black—save the scarlet headband tied around his head of long raven hair.

Antonio Valdar, his serape crisscrossed by bandoliers, stood between the two other men, staring and grinning. Andres Baliador, poised at Valdar's side, grinned with a solitary, decaying tooth on his upper gum. On the other side, the one in black, Beshkah, named for the silver plates that covered the toes of his shoes and the razor-sharp rowels on his spurs, stood and glared.

Valdar appraised the family with reptile eyes that never blinked just the same. Pang knew that Valdar and his men frequently visited the Chinese to seek the pleasure of opium, but the Lo family ran a tailoring business and did not deal in any vices. He also knew that these men gained influence by their vileness, and to break up a moment of family intimacy would be very soothing to their deviant minds. They were the most frightening men he had ever seen, with a presence like nothing short of a dooming storm.

Pang figured that his father understood the intentions of

the men immediately, even before Pang jumped from his pillow. He was thankful that his father held him back.

Valdar walked toward the table. "Ah, *compadres*, I was right." He stared at the two women who remained seated with their heads bowed. "There *are* flowers growing in this tent."

He stepped closer to them. Reached over to Sai Min and rubbed his fingertips down her powdery cheek.

The muscles in Pang's jaw tightened. "She is to be my wife!"

Hingon clenched his hand tighter around his son's arm.

Valdar looked squarely at Pang and let out a scoffing laugh. He grabbed a clear bottle of tequila from Baliador and took several large swallows. He smacked and licked his lips. "Your wife, eh?"

He grabbed Sai Min by the arm and jerked her to him. She gasped with fear and tried not to show her face.

Pang wanted badly to stop this humiliation, but his arm was locked in his father's grasp, and he could only vent his fury by exhaling large breaths of air.

Valdar laughed again and pushed Sai Min toward his comrades. Baliador grabbed her and shoved her to the ground.

The bandit leader picked up Sai Min's pillow and tossed it away. She bowed her head toward the table as he plopped down next to her. He grabbed her chin and turned her head toward his face, drawing a gasp of fear from her lungs. Without looking away he took another drink.

Hingon addressed the men, with the calm grace that Pang had always admired.

"What do you want from us?" Hingon asked. "We have no opium"

"Aye, there is more to life than opium, *viejo*," Valdar said, rubbing a knuckle down Mun Lo's cheek.

Hingon maintained a steady composure, breathing heavily in through his nose while he continued to hold Pang's arm.

Valdar snapped his fingers, and Baliador rose and came to him with a long and narrow box. Valdar placed the box on the table and opened it, revealing a silver-and-porcelain opium pipe. Though handsomely made, the pipe represented all that was bad in this world. From a tailor's perspective, it was like a needle of destruction, and the smoke it created the thread that sewed seams of ruin through the blood of those who inhaled it.

Valdar removed the glass globe from the oil lamp and stuck the end of a chopstick into the flame. The dry wood ignited quickly, and Valdar brought the flame to the pipe and inhaled. He removed his fingertip from the porcelain damper and held the smoke in his lungs for several seconds, then blew it toward the roof of the tent. He took several more tokes, and before long his eyes became gray and rheumy.

He handed the pipe to Mun Lo, and she accepted it with trembling hands. He tipped back the tequila and watched her. His eyes peered over the bottle as if he were in a trance. When he removed the bottle from his lips, a trickle ran down his chin. He looked at Mun Lo with a befuddled smile then grabbed her by the arm and jerked her to him.

As before, Pang wanted to go to her aid, but his father continued to restrain him. Pang did not understand, with their special talent for self-defense, why they could not stop this atrocity. Kung fu was something that the people of this country did not know, and Pang had always believed it was their special weapon. But Hingon continued to hold back, and even when Pang looked at him, he responded only with a discreet shake of his head.

Pang just stood there, his muscles as tight as piano strings while these men invaded their home and challenged their integrity. He watched them all carefully, especially Baliador, who kneeled and clutched the arm of his fiancée.

Baliador looked back at him through black, squinted eyes. A long, narrow mustache hung over his chin at both ends, and his thin face, like the others', was sweaty and dark from many days in the sun.

Unlike Baliador, Beshkah paid no attention to Pang. He sat on the floor beside Sai Min. The silver of his shoes and spurs reflected the dull light as he held the ivory end of a bamboo pipe to his lips and sucked in the smoke. Then Pang watched the bandit's hand as it moved under Sai Min's robe.

Mun Lo screamed as Valdar ripped open her robe and licked her neck. He let out a coarse laugh then took another drink. This time Pang could feel a different tension in his father's grasp, as if this wise old man had reached the peak of his tolerance. But when Valdar stood and pushed Mun Lo away, Hingon kept his stance.

Valdar called out to his men. *"Vayamos, hombres."*

Baliador stood quickly, but Beshkah was a little more hesitant and kept kissing Sai Min's ear. Valdar walked to him and kicked one of his shoes.

*"Vayamos!"*

Beshkah grunted angrily and pushed Sai Min away.

Valdar came back to Mun Lo, grabbed her by the arm, and lifted her to her feet. Beshkah grabbed Sai Min in the same manner. The two women screamed and cowered.

Hingon stepped in front of his son and confronted Valdar. "Why do you do this to my family?"

"What is wrong, *viejo*? Do you not like to see us enjoy ourselves?"

"Please, leave our home. We have done nothing to you."

"Maybe we *will* leave. And maybe we will take something with us."

Pang broke loose from his father's grasp, and this time Hingon did not stop him. Valdar pulled a revolver from under his serape and pointed it at Pang. No one moved.

"Ah," Valdar said. "You know that no one can stop us, right?"

"My daughters have done nothing to you," Hingon said. "Leave them. I will give you everything I have."

"That is very kind of you, but these fine young women are worth more than anything you have."

"Please, I beg you."

"Do not beg, *viejo*. It's something I cannot bear to watch."

Valdar and his comrades laughed wildly as they dragged the screaming women out of the tent. Hingon and Pang ran after them, but Valdar turned and shot his revolver, forcing them to refrain.

Hingon fell backward and collapsed into his son's arms. Pang lowered him to the ground, observed his narrowing eyes, then a spot of blood that grew on the white cotton robe over his chest.

Pang put his hand on the side of his father's face.

"Father?"

Hingon's jaw quivered and his mouth opened. "Have faith, my son. For the justice you desire, do not pay with blood, but with service to your people."

After a lengthy exhale between his lips, Hingon's eyes closed, and Pang looked up into the sky and from the bottom of his lungs cried for the soul of his father.

The gunshot had brought out the neighboring Chinese from their homes, one of them a special friend to the Los, Vin Long, who came quickly to Hingon's side. Pang embraced his father, reciting a Chinese prayer that asked for protection of Hingon's spirit.

Vin placed a hand on Pang's shoulder. "Peace will one day belong to us, but by the grace of He who is more powerful, your father will never know the wicked again."

Pang looked up at him with a bitter stare. "Take his body and prepare it for burial."

"You do not need to ask twice. I will be at your service."

Pang looked out to the end of the street, to where the gaslights faded away. "And if it kills me, *I will* be a service to my people."

The Chinese had been in Tucson less than a decade, and little had changed other than that they now had the ability to form a separate community. Pang's father, like Vin, had once worked for the Southern Pacific Railroad, and during a shutdown period in the severe heat of July, he came to Tucson rather than waiting out the downtime or returning to Mother China.

He and Vin went into business, his father starting a tailoring trade and Vin a restaurant. The start-up was difficult, as they weren't welcome anywhere they tried to settle. They were thought of as filthy heathens and faced humiliating and often brutal resistance wherever they landed. But Hingon and Vin were clear-minded and knew that because of the poverty back in the Guangdong Province, made worse by the Opium Wars, they could not have a better life than what they could gain here. If possible they would make their fortune and take it back with them, or else they would send for their families. When the time came, they would do whichever seemed more feasible.

But now, to Pang, it all seemed to have been in vain. He remembered how happy he was when his father had arranged for his sister to join them in this place called America. They could not afford to bring their mother for another year, and the special gift was to be that she would be there for Pang and Sai Min's wedding.

Pang had to be the one to deliver the sad news of his father's death to his mother, and by letter, not in person. With all that he now faced, he feared he would never see her again either.

He left his father's body to Vin and walked steadily toward the railroad tracks, out of the Chinese district. He was certain that the gunshot was heard on the other side, but no attention was ever given to their part of town, their people, unless it was to the gain of the whites.

No gaslights were near the tracks, so he walked a short distance in total darkness, destined to the street ahead, where lights on the poles glowed again and where the saloons gave off the only signs of activity.

He walked up onto the planked sidewalk and under the awning, past two doors to an adobe building with windows guarded by iron bars. The door was locked, so he gazed down a ways and across the street at the glow that came through the windows and above the batwing doors of the saloon. Laughing, hollering, and music from the building polluted the serenity of the night. Chinese weren't allowed to enter the saloons. Havoc sure stirred if ever it happened, and it rarely did. Pang credited the wisdom for the avoidance of such trouble to his elders, but there were those stray few with a death wish. Pang wondered if he suddenly had one of his own.

Nothing could stop his drive. He felt no fear and walked on, diagonally across the dusty street to the walkway in front of the saloon. He peered through the window at the many patrons sitting at the poker and faro tables, with saloon girls at their side or on their lap, encouraging their bets with drink, gartered thighs, and cleavage. A man sat at a piano while a woman watched him and played a white man's tune Pang didn't know. He didn't know any, and didn't want to. All he wanted now was to find the sheriff, and he found him leaned up at the bar sharing a laugh with a well-dressed man.

Pang took a deep breath and walked up to the doors. A man came through, bumped into Pang, and nearly fell down, but he caught himself and looked the young Chinaman over, then shook his head and said, "No, no, can't be . . . ," and turned and staggered into the street.

Pang looked over the doors and with another breath pushed through them. The first to notice him was a dealer at a poker table, then the woman at the piano, who lost her smile and tapped the player on the shoulder. The music stopped and the player turned around. Most of the patrons looked at the player first, but then turned around to see what had captured his interest.

All eyes looked at Pang.

Though they were all interested in him, he was only interested in one man, the sheriff, Chas Dutton.

The bartender, on the other side of the bar, between Dutton and the well-dressed man, reached below and pulled up a short club. Dutton turned from the bar and stood straight. The well-dressed man eyeballed Pang as if waiting for a reaction.

"You're not allowed in here and you know it," Dutton said.

Pang stood firm. "I wish to speak to you."

The sheriff glanced around at the crowd then back at Pang. "Yeah, and I wish every time I drank whiskey that I could piss gold." The crowd guffawed.

"My father was killed by Antonio Valdar. Just now, outside our home. And he has taken my sister and fiancée with him."

Pang knew that name would get the sherrif's attention, and the crowd's, and it did. They all took turns glancing at one another, and Dutton took a quick look at the floor. Valdar was not just an enemy to the Chinese, but to everyone. He would be gunned down the instant he set foot in town, but he rarely did. He usually only went to the Chinese district, where white men rarely went, and to the lone villages in the wilderness where he'd commit his vile acts and be long gone before a posse could ever form. There were wanted signs up all over Tucson for him, and for his two sidekicks—$500 for Valdar and $100 each for Baliador and Beshkah.

"I can't help you," Dutton said. "Now, you go back before there's trouble."

"I will not leave. Valdar is near and I know the direction

he went." Pang scanned over all the patrons. "And I know there are many of you who would like the rewards. Now is your chance."

He could tell they pondered his words, but no one jumped. The only movement came from Dutton as he stepped toward Pang, his spurs jingling on the wooden floor.

"You're way out of line here, Chinaman." He stopped only a few steps from Pang, both his hands on his waist. "Now I said git and I mean it!"

To Pang's left, Deputy Bain spun out of his chair and stood. He was simply dressed, in homespun trousers, a gray band-collared shirt, and a battered derby with a star pinned to the crown. He also wore a holstered gun around his hips, the holster tied to the bottom of his thigh with a leather string.

Dutton nodded to the deputy, who went for Pang with his arm raised. Pang reacted with a quick spin, jabbing his hand into the back of the deputy's neck and sending him sailing into a table of patrons. Cards, coins, jewelry, and paper notes flew onto the floor as the deputy sprawled across the table.

Pang stood there in a wide stance, his knees bent, arms raised over his chest, hands elongated, eyes glaring.

The people at the table helped the deputy up. Now hatless, he came back at Pang, only to catch a foot in his chest and another hand across the back of his neck.

"Enough!" yelled Dutton, who now had his gun drawn and pointed at Pang.

The deputy lay on the floor and wheezed.

"This is your final warning," Dutton said. "Either you leave or you're going down to the jail. And I promise you it won't be a fun night after what you just did to the jail keeper."

"I'm not going anywhere until someone goes after Valdar."

Dutton nodded at two more men, who closed in on Pang. The young Chinaman held up his hands as both of them approached. The deputy rose slowly from the floor. Dutton cocked the hammer back on his pistol. "It's your choice. You touch another one of my men, I shoot you where you stand."

"Then I will go to your jail. I will not leave your presence until you do what you're sworn to do."

"Now, you listen here and you listen good. I won't tolerate that kind of talk out of no one, I don't care who they are or where they come from. You try any more of that fancy dancin' around me or my men, or keep talkin' that smart talk, and you'll be growin' old in my jail. You hearin' me?"

Pang stood straight and crossed his arms. The two men grabbed him, one at each side, and the deputy punched Pang's stomach. The young Chinaman winced and curled to the floor. The deputy drew a fist and hit him across the jaw, and while he lay on the floor, he kicked Pang in the chest.

"All right, that's enough," Dutton said.

The deputy looked angrily back at the sheriff, but the men picked Pang up and dragged him out the door. Dutton holstered his gun, and his spurs clanged as he followed them. They had no more than stepped into the street when all the musical sounds of the saloon played again and made Tucson seem like a town of innocence.

# ENRIQUE OSORIO

Darkness covered the desert when Enrique woke, and he wondered if it all hadn't been a bad dream, but then he smelled the blood of his parents on his hands. He felt hopeless, and though he had never experienced anything so frightening and painful, he always thought of his grandfather during times of loneliness. The father of his mother, a resourceful man, who built their adobe and with a two-wheeled cart brought the pine logs down from the mountains to make their corral. He was the one who taught Enrique most of what he knew about the wilderness and how to hunt, and who always had the right thing to say about anything that troubled the boy. His *abuelo*, Isidro Jesus de la Rosa, was the greatest man Enrique had ever known, and he wished for the warmth of his presence.

Enrique had been told stories of curses on people and that things like this had often happened to those cursed, and

he wondered if now his family were suffering such consequences. No, they had done nothing to deserve this. They
were good people, who made friends with the Tohono
O'odham and certain bands of Apache, and the gringos that
came through to California or had now settled in nearby
Tucson. Enrique's family were farmers, who irrigated the
land to grow their crops and raised livestock that not only
fed their families but helped feed others. They were even
blessed by a priest, Father Gaeta, from a mission in Tuma-
cacori, who visited often and helped in the fields and took
back with him gifts of food from Enrique's mother. They
lived a peaceful life, and it was unjust that such tragedy
should fall on the family.

A coyote howled and then a pack of them yipped. The
coyotes had long been neighbors to Enrique and his family,
and their cries were like nighttime music. It was nice to have
that familiar sound, but it was not nearly enough to ease the
hollowness he now felt.

The boy lay on the cool ground and tried to imagine what
he would do after this great tragedy. He kept thinking
about Amelia and wondering if she had escaped that ugly
man. Maybe she got away and ran back to their home and
found their parents dead, and the dead Apache. Did he really
kill him? Maybe she got scared and was now out in the
desert hiding or looking for him. But what if the ugly man
killed her? The thought made Enrique close his eyes tight
and hold his breath, trying to keep back the emotion that
swelled in his chest.

It had been more than two years since his grandfather
had left for El Paso, where he went to care for his ailing
brother. He told Enrique that he would return very soon and

that he would take him up to the mountains to camp and hunt the black-tailed deer. He had anxiously awaited his elder's return, wanting to show him how accomplished he had become as a man of the wilderness. But his longing was different now. Because he did not know the fate of his sister, his grandfather might be his only living relative, and he was so far away.

Enrique drifted to sleep again and in his dreams saw the faces of the desperate, merciless men. He saw them so clearly, as if he were nose to nose with each of them, the sweating face of the man who hurt Amelia, the man with shiny shoes who chased him with a knife, and the bare-chested Apache with his rounded eyes and screaming, blood-soaked face. It was that man in his last, dying breath who grabbed the boy by the throat and squeezed until he could not breathe. Enrique grabbed the man's wrist, but it was as if an iron claw had hold of him and the only existence in the world was blood, fear, and death.

He woke sitting upright and holding his throat with his own hands. He let loose quickly and stared at his hands as if they were something not to be trusted. He backed against the rocks in fear and crossed his arms over his chest, hugging himself and wondering when this all would end.

He heard a dove and looked up into the sky and saw that day was breaking. A new day was coming and he knew not how it would begin. On a normal day he would help his father round up the goats for milking. Amelia would feed the chickens while their mother fixed breakfast of eggs cooked with peppers and chicken and wrapped in a tortilla. *Huevos con pimientas y pollo en una tortilla*, his favorite. Normally the thought of it would make his stomach rumble with hunger, but now it felt tightened into a knot and he could not possibly eat. But his mouth was dry, and he decided it would be good to find water. He was too afraid to go back to his home, so he decided to drink from a cluster of barrel cactus, using a method that his grandfather had taught him, of poking a hole with one of the cactus thorns, then curling a yucca leaf and letting the water flow down the furrowed leaf into his mouth.

The water was sweet and refreshing, and it would do for now. The cactus was plentiful in the desert, so he was not concerned about going without. It was not yet time for the summer monsoons, when the Sonora received most of its rain, filling the creeks and rivers, but the winter snow that had melted and flowed down the mountains was still nurturing the ground, providing the necessary nutrition for the spring plant life to bloom. Though the cacti sprouted many flowers this time of year, and it was normally a vibrant image of life in the Sonora, Enrique could only sense the ways of evil. His parents were dead, the whereabouts of his sister unknown, and his grandfather far, far way. He was all alone, and all because of ruthless, desperate men.

He found the trail that led to the area where he'd last seen Amelia, and he walked cautiously. He looked for footprints and saw where she and the man both had walked into the arroyo—the stirring of the sand where the strange behavior had occurred, and the tracks out, which consisted of one set of large prints and another of drag marks. Though it appeared that the man had dragged his sister, he saw no blood or any other traces that she might be dead, so he could not be certain.

He walked on and followed the trail, fearful that at any

moment the man and his sweaty face would look right down at him. When he realized that the trail was leading back to his home, he stopped and pondered getting any closer. He supposed he could approach slowly, creep on his hands and knees, and lie low if he saw movement. He could think of nothing else to do. There was nowhere to go, other than the mountains, to hide, but the nights there would still be cold, and he did not want to build fires that someone could see, or cause smoke that someone could smell. He also thought about going to find his grandfather. Though he did not know how to get to El Paso, he was certain he could find the way. But the one unanswered question was the fate of Amelia. He could not bear to go away without knowing if she were dead or alive. What if she needed help? He would look for her, even if it took his lifetime to do so, and he would find her. If she were dead, he would give her a proper burial, and pray for her like Father Gaeta would do. If he could not find her, he would go to El Paso and find his grandfather, and together they would look for her.

Enrique crawled to where he could peek around an agave plant, and saw a lone chicken pecking the ground. The stable stood distinct and barren, the only dwelling left in its original state. A haze of gray smoke hovered above the roof- less and charred adobe, a portion of one wall collapsed into rubble. Flies swarmed and vultures ripped at the flesh of the goat corpses that after a day in the sun lay bloated by the desert heat. From where he lay he could not see the bodies of his parents, and he wondered if the men had buried them. But no, it was not likely that such men would do any honor- able thing.

Enrique mulled over what to do, whether to go look

through the remnants of their home for signs of Amelia, or to look for her departing trail. He supposed it would be best to search the home area, that if she was alive, maybe she was hiding in the stable, or, God forbid, if she was dead, they might have left her somewhere near the adobe. The thought of it all tore at his emotions. But he was a man now. If he found her dead, he would then make three graves for all his family. Difficult for sure, but it was something a man must do.

Staying low, he crept closer and was immediately sickened when he saw that vultures also perched on and tore at the corpses of his mother and father. He closed his eyes and held his head low, feeling deep sorrow for his loving family. Something he couldn't bear anymore—he stood and yelled. The vultures lifted their heavy wings and glided away, landing only a short distance from the bodies. Enrique picked up rocks and threw them at the unsightly birds.

"Get away, you ugly scavengers! Damn you!"

It felt awkward to curse, especially since it was something that he had never done, and had only heard from the tongues of grown men. But he *was* a man now, on his own, and the world seemed against him. If cursing would make him stronger, he would have to use it.

The air seemed suddenly silent, and Enrique realized that he had exposed himself to anyone who might be around. But no one came about, so he walked into the scene. The vultures didn't go far, but Enrique was certain that with him there they would not return, and that his parents would be buried before they could get to them, so deep into the ground that even the coyotes couldn't get the scent and *Mamá* and *Papá* would rest in peace.

He saw no fresh tracks near the stable, or none that looked like Amelia's. The stable was the only place she could have hidden out of view, but she was not there. He saw a large stain of dried blood in the sand, where he'd hit the Apache with the machete, but the Apache was not there. He saw tracks leading out into the desert and a trail of dried blood. The Apache would surely die, if not by bleeding to death, by an animal that smelled his blood.

He continued looking around and found a square metal blade that his father had tied to a short wooden pole and used as a shovel. The handle was partially burned and charred and difficult for Enrique to hold, but he took it anyway and found a place not far away from the adobe to begin digging.

The sand was hard and crusty on top, and darker and moist as he dug further. There were many rocks that slowed the process. He tried to scoop and pry them out with the shovel, but many could only be loosened and had to be dug out with his fingers. He hadn't dug very much before his arm felt tight and fatigued, and after assessing his work he realized that he knew nothing about digging graves, that this deed was something that would take him hours if not days to complete. But if he was really a man, he would have to do this, so he kept digging, occasionally stopping to rub his arms.

The vultures tried to come back, but he stood and shooed them away, cursed them, then went back to his digging. Eventually he became so tired that he had no more strength to continue breaking dirt. He rested his head against the shovel blade. His blistered, blackened hands could no longer grip the charcoal-laden handle. Feeling defeated, he fell to the ground, but now that he was a man, he would not permit himself to cry.

He wasn't sure how long he lay there, but he felt disoriented and sleepy. He fell backward and looked up into the clear and pale blue sky, with the rays of the sun making yellow circles that ran back to their origin like a string of glowing beads. He watched the dots change directions, the smaller ones far away, and the larger ones closer, but always staying together. He wondered if they would always be that way, if like humans and some animals they slept at night and came back out in the day to hang down from the sun and spread light over the desert. But then he saw a face appear among the dots, and he wondered if they were really angels, coming down to claim the souls of his parents. He heard the bray of a donkey and felt sure that angels did not ride donkeys. When the face spoke, he wondered what kind of tricks the sky was playing on him.

"Are you okay, son?"

The face came closer, and a hand touched Enrique's forehead. Water was dabbed on his tongue and then arms picked him up and carried him. It was all making sense now. The circles of light *were* angels, and this one was taking him to heaven to be with his family.

Enrique hadn't seen Father Gaeta in several months. It was winter the last time the priest had made his rounds to spread the love of God along the foothills and the bank of the Santa Cruz River. Enrique's father didn't pay much attention to him—thought of him more as a nuisance than anything, coming around distracting them with silly talk when there was much work to do. But his mother adored the young priest. Being a descendant of Spanish conquistadores, she decorated a wall of their home with a cross, and a rosary was always close at hand.

Even though Father Gaeta wasn't a Catholic, Jesuit, or even a Franciscan, but a priest who followed his own unique faith, Enrique's mother felt especially blessed when he came to see them; as if God Himself were now closer to them. But the boy's *papá*, a Tohono O'odham, would never be converted. He would say, "If God is only present when the priest comes around, then we are as doomed as a lame rabbit." His *mamá* would make the cross over her chest then shoo him away from her. He would grin and wink at Enrique.

Now that they were dead, Enrique wondered if his *papá* wasn't right, or if there was even a God at all.

"Are you not hungry, Enrique?" the priest said.

The boy hadn't realized he was merely twirling his spoon in his soup bowl, daydreaming. He brought the spoon to his mouth and sipped. Though he had never had soup made with peas, corn, and yellow squash, and slivers of chicken meat, he liked the taste. But the broth was more appealing and easier for him to swallow.

Father Gaeta broke off a piece of bread, dipped it in the soup, and bit off the soggy end. The boy still did not have the stomach for such a filling meal and only drank the broth. The tragedy kept rolling around in his mind, from the point where it began, seeing the bandits amid their craziness, to the point where he woke from sleep at the mission. He wondered how such a horrible situation could take place if a priest were nearby.

He studied the priest while he ate, as if to look for something magical, or maybe fake. "Why were you coming to see us, Father?"

The priest swallowed his food and smiled at the boy. "It's foresummer, my son. Time for the saguaro fruit harvest. I thought your father would like some help."

The boy thought for a moment. "So you weren't bringing God to us?"

The priest laughed. His healthy white teeth were an ivory glow amid his long brown beard. "Oh, my dear boy. God is everywhere. Why would you ask such a question?"

Enrique twirled his spoon again, half his thoughts in sadness, the other half in disgust.

Father Gaeta adopted a solemn gaze, took the last bite of his bread, brushed his hands together, and nodded to the boy. "I understand," he said as he chewed.

"I don't."

"Well, son, my heart sank when I found you there, exhausted after dutifully digging the graves for your parents. Never have I seen so much heart in a young lad." He watched the boy sip at his soup. "Your *mamá* and *papá* would have been proud of you, Enrique."

"But I didn't get to bury them, you did."

"That does not matter. You gave it your all, and God sent me there to help you fulfill your honor."

Enrique dropped the spoon in the bowl and tried to hold back his emotion. This made no sense. It felt wrong. Why couldn't the father have come earlier and saved his family?

"If there is a God, how could he do these things to my family?" the boy asked.

"Those bandits made their own choices, Enrique. God didn't."

"But you always told us he was all-powerful, and that we were good people, and that God would protect us."

The priest sighed. "I know I did, son."

"Then why did this happen? You lied to us!"

The priest rose from the table, reached for the boy's hand, and squatted beside him. "No, Enrique, listen. It is sometimes very difficult to understand God's motives. The meek, and those who suffer by the hands of the wicked, will find paradise in His kingdom. But we must not ever doubt Him. And, my son, I do believe that God has a special plan for you. That is why you survived all this."

The boy could only stare at the priest, wondering how any of his ideas could be trusted.

The father rose again to his feet. "Why don't you come with me?"

Enrique stood slowly, took Father Gaeta's hand, and followed. They walked together out of the mission, into the bright sunny day and toward the bank of the Santa Cruz River. The river was experiencing a dry time and was very shallow. The priest let go of Enrique's hand and stepped out into the dull current in his sandaled feet. He stood there, looking back, the tail of his brown robe absorbing the water.

"Enrique, do you know what it means to be baptized?"

The boy only stared nervously and did not understand.

The priest gazed down at the water. "I've baptized many in this river. Whites, Indians, Mexicans, *Criollos*. *Vitae spiritualis ianua*. Baptism . . . it is the beginning of life with God and Christ. Through baptism we are freed from sin and reborn as children of God."

Enrique looked down at the water. "If I would have been

baptized, would those bad things have happened to my family?"

"Oh, my son, this life will always bring hard times. It's the life after this one that brings us peace. But we have to accept Christ first, and be baptized. Maybe someday you would like to give it a try?"

The boy looked hard at the priest. "No, I don't think I want to."

"Enrique, I want to protect your soul, and for you to give it to God. That way, if anything ever happens to you, like what happened to your family, you will not die, but find a better life in heaven. And there, you will meet all your family again."

The boy liked the idea of being able to see his family again, but his desire for justice churned his blood more. "Nothing is going to happen to me. I am going to kill those men who killed my family."

The priest came back to the bank and put his hand gently on top of Enrique's head. "My dear boy, you must always understand that vengeance belongs to God."

"Then why doesn't he kill them?"

"You should not worry so much about the death of others, but about your own life."

"I can't think of anything else."

"I know this is hard for you, but for the sake of your own soul you must try to make things right for yourself."

Enrique could not feel what the priest wanted him to feel. He wanted to see the men dead, screaming and bloody, like they had left his parents. It was the only way he could see his justice.

Father Gaeta looked out to the water, then turned back to the boy. "You're right. You should not be pressured to God. Let's take a walk."

Enrique moped behind, and eventually they stood side by side and the priest squinted as he looked up at the mission tower.

Unlike the simple adobes and other *rancherio* shelters found throughout the Sonora, it was a structure with thick walls and an arched façade and molded columns lining the entrance. The bell tower stood to the side of the nave, two stories taller.

"You know," the priest said, "this mission has never had a bell in its tower."

"Why not?"

"They ran out of money. Sun-fired brick and Indian labor were not as hard to obtain. But when Friar Ramon ran out of funds, just the building had to be enough."

"Was Friar Ramon your friend?"

"No, he was before my time. A Franciscan. They left here a few years after Mexico won its independence from Spain. The missions were no longer supported by the government."

Enrique thought for a moment. "If God is so great, why does He need the government?"

Father Gaeta looked down at Enrique and smiled. "You are a bright young man. No, the main purpose of these missions was not to convert the Indians to Christianity, as many have thought, but more so to make taxpaying citizens out of them. Regardless of what they tried to make people believe, it wasn't so much about saving souls."

"Then why are you here, Father?"

"Ah, that is the difference in our purpose. I *am* here to

save souls. If anything, to keep peace among the people. Keep them neighborly and from mutilating one another."

Enrique thought about how his own family had been ruthlessly murdered. "How can you do that? You didn't save my family."

The priest knelt before Enrique. "My dear boy. I am just a mortal man, like you. Like your father. I do not have the power, as God would have, to prevent such horrible things from happening. I am merely a representative of God, and operate from my own free will, with His spirit working through me."

He stood and put his arm around Enrique, and they walked behind the mission and into the garden. "That is what my visits to the villages are all about. I like to bring smiles and fellowship to my neighbors, no matter what their beliefs may be. No, I am not a true Catholic. I'd have been banned from the church years ago. I follow my own beliefs, and that is mostly to free a man's soul from hate and greed. They are the most deadly elements a man can carry."

"You are not a Christian?"

"On the contrary! I believe entirely in Christ. It's just the religions created by man I question."

The priest looked to the garden and pointed down at a row of plants. "Maize. See it?"

"Yes," Enrique said, drooping his head. "My mother grew it, too."

The priest continued pointing. "And there are melons . . . squash there, and dragon's claw. As you can see, I irrigate from the Santa Cruz. One of the things I liked about this mission. One could survive here *and* serve God."

A rustling noise came from a creosote bush behind them. They both turned and looked, Enrique a bit startled.

"Is that you, Sereno?" the priest said.

A small boy, with long black hair and a red headband, and eyes darker than Enrique's, peered around the bush.

"Who is he?" Enrique said.

"He's an orphan of a Tohono O'odham family, who I feed, and then he leaves. He must be hungry. I call him Sereno because he is always watching."

"Will he come and talk to us?"

"I'm not sure he can, even if he wanted to. He's been coming around here for over a year. His family was killed in an Apache raid and his throat was cut. But it wasn't a lethal wound. I'm certain it affected his voice."

"How do you know all this?" Enrique asked.

I found him in the desert shortly after the attack. I could see the blood on his neck. He wouldn't let me get close to him. So I left him some bread. I tended to the dead, and then took food to him each day. One day I decided to quit spoiling him and see if I could lure him here. It wasn't long before he started coming here for the food."

"Where does he eat now?"

The priest pointed to the other side of the garden.

"I leave the food in the stable behind the mission, but only after the stable has been cleaned."

"Who cleans it?"

The priest grinned. "Sereno, of course."

Enrique thought for a moment. "But how did he know?"

"He may not speak, but he hears, and he understands. He came one day and expected food but found a pitchfork instead. That's when he realized that he must earn his keep. I came back later and the stable was clean, and I left him bread, a plate of stew, and a cup of milk. Ever since then he has come in and cleans the stable, then I leave his supper."

Enrique looked back and forth, at the dark-eyed boy peeking out at them and at the stable.

"I could offer you the same, you know," the priest said.

Enrique looked up at him.

"You could stay here," said the priest, "help out in the garden, with the goats, and tend to the burros and chickens. Does that interest you?"

Enrique shrugged, thinking of his home, now in shambles. "I don't know."

"In return I will give you a place to sleep, feed you, and teach you to read, write, and do arithmetic. What do you say?"

"I don't want those things. I have to go to El Paso."

"What is in El Paso?"

"My grandfather. He went there two years ago. Said his brother was sick and needed him. Well I need him now. With his help I will find Amelia, and together we can find and kill those men."

"Do you not know who those men are, Enrique?"

"Two Apache and one a mixed gringo. I thought I killed one, but I am not sure now."

"I see. Well, my son, I'm certain the men that raided your home are the gang of Antonio Valdar. They will not go down easy. So you must be stronger and wiser, which means nutrition, and an education."

"That will help?"

The priest sighed. "It would be a beginning."

"Then you will help me?"

"I will help you be a better man, Enrique."

Enrique's yearning to leave for El Paso was paramount, but for some reason the boy felt the need to stick around the mission for a while. Maybe it was the priest's promises of helping him become a better man. The boy liked being called a man.

"Okay. I will stay awhile."

Father Gaeta put his arm around Enrique's neck. "All right then! For now, why don't we go fix Sereno's supper?"


Enrique's daily life along the Santa Cruz River had become routine, which frightened him, and he tried not to think about it. Though he enjoyed his duties—caring for the twenty goats, milking the does, feeding the chickens, gathering the eggs, getting water from the river, or hunting wild game for food—whenever he began to feel content, it was like a prompt to put up a front against his happiness. He was too afraid that if he loved what was around him too much, it would all disappear.

When these feelings came about him, he had learned to exercise his brain, to go on to something else. Such as during the saguaro fruit harvest, which reminded him so much of his family, but the priest told him that the memories of his family, good and bad, would never fade, so he might as well learn to live with them. It was good though, he also said, not to dwell on things and to move on. Enrique would think about his schooling, which he looked forward to each day. His lessons in biology, of the plants and animals in the Sonora, were quite enjoyable. The priest was impressed with how much Enrique already knew, and the boy assured him it was because of his grandfather.

"He must be a great man," the priest said, with a consoling hand to Enrique's shoulder. It was another moment when the boy preferred to go on to something else.

Not only did the priest teach Enrique to read and write, but he taught him English as well as Spanish. The boy liked learning English, as he had always wanted to know what those drummers on the trail were saying. He remembered how frustrated they were trying to communicate with his parents, who didn't know English. It wouldn't have mattered anyway. Regardless of how much his mother liked the things the men were trying to sell, they didn't have the money for them. Even if they had, his father would not have let her buy them.

The boy's lessons in arithmetic were past the basics and were now mostly exercised with random quizzes by Father Gaeta.

"Enrique," the priest would say as the boy carried water from the river. "How do you calculate the volume of water inside that clay pot?"

"The easy way, Father, or the hard way?"

The priest laughed. "The easy way, of course."

"I pour the water out of the odd-shaped pot and into a perfectly square crock. Then I calculate the volume of a cube."

"Very good, my son."

Father Gaeta made Enrique's lessons enjoyable, which helped him learn. Though the priest didn't have many books, the boy read sparingly from what was there, and not too much at once—such as the Holy Bible. Enrique often read and reread the book of Job, the Song of Solomon, and the prophets, such as Jeremiah, Daniel, Jonah, or his favorite, Nahum, the comforter, who gave a message of judgment, and a verse that Enrique had memorized:

> *Keep your feasts, O Judah, fulfill your vows,*
> *for never again shall the wicked come against*
> *you, he is utterly cut off.*

Though there was little in the priest's library, Enrique enjoyed what was there, which consisted of a two-century-old book on learning by Sir Francis Bacon that he thought to be rather pompous and, at times, off track and boring. There was a book of Scottish poems, partially burned, that Father Gaeta said he'd acquired from a settlement that had been ransacked by Apaches, but its content was touching, nonetheless; and another favorite was a tattered copy of Benjamin Franklin's *Poor Richard's Almanac*. Enrique liked the verse, mostly for its clever wit. He often thought that if reading were like sustenance, then the Holy Bible would be the main course of a meal and the *Almanac* like a sweet dessert.

He liked his duties, and enjoyed his education, but what he loved most was his time alone in the wilderness. Every day he would find his favorite spot on top of a bluff overlooking an arroyo and a deer trail. Not only would he see deer, but also many other animals and birds, such as kangaroo rats, pronghorn, coyote, gray fox, ringtail, coati, quail, and porcupine, but he was there for the deer.

Sereno always accompanied Enrique on his hunts, too. On his first hunt away from the mission, Enrique sat upon the rise overlooking a bend in the deer trail. Usually before he ever saw the deer, he would hear a strange whistle, one that sounded like a rare bird, but nothing at all like any of the birds in the Sonora. It was more than a coincidence that the whistle came shortly before deer came around the bend, and once Enrique had figured it out, he started looking for Sereno somewhere among the desert plants, hiding but watching. He rarely ever saw his *amigo sombra*, his shadow friend, but the first time he did was also the only time he'd ever seen Sereno smile.

Father Gaeta had shown Enrique how to use a bow and arrow, a gift the priest received from a friendly Apache chief. Enrique was fascinated with the weapon. The bow, made from the wood of a mulberry tree, was painted on the inside by a red dye, and a golden dye colored the outside. An emblem of the sun was also painted on the inside, in the same gold color, laid on top of the red.

The arrows, which Enrique had to learn to make, were made of the same mulberry wood. He used a method that the priest had taught him, which the priest said he was also shown by the Apache. Every time the boy went to the wilderness, he looked for mulberry trees, and would break off small limbs and take them back to the mission. At the mission he would cut the limbs to approximately two-foot lengths, remove the bark, and scrape the wood, then lay them in the sun to dry. The Apache arrows that were given to him were decorated with black, red, and blue stripes, but Enrique just used red dye, the color of blood, which also symbolized the color of the justice that lingered in the back of his mind.

Feathers could be obtained from red-tailed hawks or eagles, and sometimes buzzards, but Enrique was superstitious about using feathers from a scavenger and relied solely on the others. When he found the feathers—and sometimes he would find a complete dead bird—he would cut the quill down the center, scrape out the marrow, and cut the feather into five-inch lengths. He would store the lengths in a leather pouch until it came time to make new arrows. He'd attach the feathers with wet sinew and piñon pitch, another technique the Apaches had shown the priest and that was passed on to Enrique.

Arrowheads were something else that Enrique looked out for while wandering throughout the wilderness. The Apache claimed that they were left by ancestors for their descendents to find, already shaped by nature with flat and pointed edges. Enrique had found scores of arrowheads, which he kept in another leather pouch. When he made his own arrows, or repaired them, he split the end of the arrow, inserted the flat end of the head, and wrapped it with more wet sinew. But there were times when an arrow was broken and too short to add the weight of a stone or flint to the end, and was simply sharpened to a wooden point, which was just as deadly.

Enrique's quiver, which was also part of the Apache gift to the priest, was made of deerskin, as was the cover for the bow. He'd carry as many as ten arrows, along with his two pouches of feathers and arrowheads, and a coil of extra bowstrings. The bowstrings, which Enrique had to replace at times, were made from the sinew of a deer's loin, or from the legs, which he saved from every kill.

The boy practiced by shooting into a target made of deerskin stretched against plank boards he'd found at the mission. He painted a red dot the width of his hand in the center. It was difficult for him at first, not only to hit his target, but to pull the string at all. The priest assured him that carrying heavy buckets of water, and lifting them as he walked, would strengthen his arms so he could pull the bowstring like a man. This challenged the boy, and he worked his arms endlessly, and within a year he could pull the string and hit his target proficiently, even much better than the priest.

The priest often challenged Enrique, too, by sitting at the table, rolling up his sleeve, exposing a pale, wiry arm, and challenging the boy to an arm wrestle.

"Let's see if you've grown, my son," the priest would say, encouraging Enrique to try and move his arm. It was a measurement for both of them, however, not just Enrique. When the day came that he was able to move the priest's arm any distance at all, Enrique would know he was that much closer to handling the tasks of a man. The priest, Enrique knew, would also know that it was time to prepare the boy for starting his life outside the mission.

The boy had always wanted to learn all about hunting and the wilderness from his grandfather, and even though it began that way, his grandfather never taught him about hunting big game. That he learned from the priest, passed down from the Apache and Tohono O'odham, even the gutting and quartering.

One day, after a kill, Enrique was quartering the meat from a mule deer and packing it on the back of his burro when he heard a noise, and then he saw several javelina playing not far away at the base of the bluff. This was only the second time in his life he had seen these animals, and he was quite taken by their piglike appearance, with a grayish, bristly hide.

Though this sighting was somewhat treasured as a rare moment, their initial sound was almost haunting, and before long something disturbing brought Enrique to a moment of despair.

The largest of the javelinas, a boar, kept jumping on top of another, smaller one of the species. From the noise the smaller one was making, the boy could tell it did not like the activity that was taking place, and that the boar was forcing the other to play his game. There was only one other circumstance where Enrique had heard similar noises, and that was before he had seen Valdar with Amelia. The noisy grunting—he wondered if Valdar had learned those noises from a javelina, even though Enrique still did not know what it was all about.

On his return to the mission that day, Father Gaeta met Enrique to admire his kill.

"Ah, what a fine sack of meat," the priest said and patted Enrique on the back. "You have perfected the art of hunting, my son."

Enrique did not answer, only unpacked his burro and went inside the mission to put away his things. For a moment Enrique stopped and closed his eyes; then he lay down on his bed and stared up at the adobe ceiling. The priest had followed him inside, and came up to his bedside and sat at his feet.

"What is troubling you, my son?"

Enrique lay with his eyes closed. "Today I saw two javelina. *Pecari angulatus.*"

The priest smiled. "Ah, hunting is not your only strong point. You know your animals well, too."

"But there is something that I still don't understand."

"What is that, my son?"

It had been more than a year since the massacre of his family, but the scenes were always as vivid as the day they happened. He thought more, however, of Amelia and what might have become of her, though his thoughts rarely reflected any hope. It was something about which he often wondered what the priest thought, but he never had the courage to ask, in fear of hearing a hopeless answer.

Enrique opened his eyes and looked at the priest, at his full brown beard and studious green eyes. For more than a year Enrique had learned to trust those eyes, and like his grandfather, the priest had become a man whom the boy admired. He also feared getting too close, but now, more than ever, he felt the need to open up to the father.

"What do you think happened to Amelia?" the boy asked.

The priest swallowed and looked away, scratched his beard and shrugged. "I can't be sure."

Enrique kept looking at him and noticed a bit of fear in his eyes. "I've been wondering about something."

"What have you been wondering?"

"During the deer hunt, when I saw the javelinas, this boar, with tusks, jumped on the back of a smaller one. It reminded me of the last time I saw Amelia. She was with this man you call Valdar, and before I saw him, he was making very strange grunting sounds. When I saw him leading her away, I could tell she was not happy, just like the small javelina that squealed and tried to get away."

A brief silence fell between them, and the priest looked intently at Enrique.

"That is something we've never talked about in our education," the priest said. "And I apologize for that."

The boy only looked at the priest, anxiously awaiting his explanation.

The priest looked at the floor and kept rubbing his beard. "Have you ever noticed, Enrique, the power that certain animals have over others?"

"I'm not sure what you mean, Father."

"Take the eagle, for example. A rabbit is doomed if the eagle sees it with its exquisite eyesight and calculates that it can swoop down in time to grasp it in its claws before the rabbit can reach cover. And the rat has a similar power over insects, and the insects over smaller insects. But the eagle, its only predator is man, which would mean that man's only true predator is himself. The basic difference between man and animal is their ability to feel levels of emotion and consider consequences. Antonio Valdar is an evil man who cares nothing of either and thinks more like an animal. That is why he treats other humans the way that he does."

"I see what you mean," the boy said, "but what does that have to do with Amelia?"

The priest reached and put his hand on the back of Enrique's. "Do you remember when I taught you biology and the characteristics of life?"

"Yes, of course I do."

"One characteristic, reproduction, is what the javelinas were doing. They were making little javelinas. Humans do the same thing, only it is to be done with compassion and desire from both man and woman. One thing that humans can do, that animals cannot, is take the act of reproduction for pleasure, and some force it on other humans for selfish pleasure. There is no desire from the other, nor is there any compassion. It is an act of lust and not love. It is an act of evil."

"And that is what Valdar was doing to Amelia?"

"Yes, my son. I'm afraid that is right."

"What will happen to her?"

"It is hard for me to suspect, and you are very young to be told such things."

"I am old enough to see it happen, but not old enough to understand it?"

The priest sighed and gently patted the boy's forearm. "Yes, right. Well, Valdar, he looks for ways to feed his evil desires. A young, innocent girl is one of those ways. There are people who like to enslave such girls for that same self-ish pleasure and will pay money for them. Valdar has likely captured your sister to take her and sell her into such bondage."

Though Enrique trusted the priest's explanation, Amelia's fate still wasn't clear to him. He had never felt the desires or compassion that caused a man to feel that way toward a woman. Nor had he ever felt the lust that the priest spoke of, and knowing what it had done to his *hermana*, he was certain he never wanted to.

"I just hope she is okay," the boy said.

The priest tightened his lips and nodded. "I do, too, my son."

A sound of a stone hitting the windowsill prompted them to look out. The priest peered out first then Enrique joined him. Enrique spotted Sereno dashing into a stand of willow near the riverbank.

Enrique was sure that the priest had seen him, too, and

offered him a humorous mimicry of the priest's quizzing. "What are the genus and species of that varmint I see hiding among the branches?"

Father Gaeta chuckled. "That would be the ever so punctual *Orphanis hungrius*. It must be time to eat."

# PANG LO

He woke to a blurred image of Vin Long's face and to the coolness of a wet cloth on his cheek. Vin dabbed the cloth above Pang's eye, which caused him to wince at the pain. Pang closed his eyes tight and pushed Vin's hand away, then opened his eyes again and looked out into the room. Objects started to come into focus—the bricks in the wall, the iron bars.

"You were out all night," Vin said. "And now almost half the day."

Pang closed his eyes and reopened them, and tried to get a clear view of his friend. He tasted blood. "What—what happened?"

Vin dipped the cloth into a porcelain bowl then wrung out the water. "I thought they had killed you."

"Who?"

"The deputies. They brought you here from the saloon, and after the sheriff left, they beat you. You're a damn fool."

Pang recalled the incident at the saloon, and that was the last he could remember. "Am I a fool for demanding justice?"

Vin dropped the wet, wadded cloth on Pang's chest and left it there. "One does not stick one's head into a beehive and demand honey."

Pang grabbed the cloth and tried to rise up, but a quick dizziness sent him back to the cot.

"You lie still," Vin said. "You have much healing to do."

"Why does my stomach hurt so much?"

Vin took the cloth back and dropped it into the bowl. "Do not complain. Be grateful you're alive."

"I have to get up. I have to go after Valdar."

"Do not worry. A posse of more than thirty men are already after him."

"Posse?"

"Sheriff Dutton. He received word that a man had been killed south of town. He rode out with one of the deputies and found a man hanging naked from a cottonwood tree, along the bank of the Santa Cruz. His stomach was cut open and his entrails pulled to the ground."

"Who?"

"A gambler. A fancy-dressed man who was in the saloon when you went in blurting Valdar's name. So he went after Valdar and met his death. The sheriff had to act and formed a posse."

Pang tried to rise again. "I should go help him."

This time he was knocked down by both dizziness and Vin's hand. "You are more of a fool than I thought!"

"You don't know how it feels, old man!"

Vin stood angrily. "Since you are still a young man, I will forgive you for your ignorance. No, my dear Pang, you are too young to remember the Opium Wars. I watched my father's head fall off his body from the swipe of an imperial soldier's sword. Don't think that I didn't want revenge, too. But I had a wife and a newborn child. I had them to think about. Their lives and our future."

Pang was touched by the man's words and felt regret for his hasty tongue. "I meant no disrespect."

Vin patted his shoulder. "I know. Your father was a good man. You have to know he would not approve of you thinking this way."

"Yes, and it is quite a burden on my mind. But I have nothing now. A tailoring business is nothing. Without a family I am nothing. That evil bandit took everything I have."

Vin looked at Pang with a compassionate smile and put his hand on his. Perhaps, Pang thought, the old man was seeing the situation differently.

"Do you think that Dutton will stop Valdar?" Pang said.

Vin sat silently for a moment, then looked at Pang solemnly and let out a sigh. "I am not a predictor. All I know is what I see before me."

"And what do you see?"

Another sigh. "A grasshopper."

"Then tell me, what should I do?"

"It is not for me to tell you, Pang. It is for you to decide."

"I don't understand."

"You have been taught. You know the answers. You know the way. Just remember . . . a leopard stalks its prey before it attacks."

Pang thought for a moment. "Yes," he said matter-of-factly. "It does."

Vin nodded, then stood and walked to the cell door to

summon the jail keeper. Deputy Bain approached with his spurs clanging and keys jingling. He looked through the bars and grinned smugly at Pang, then unlocked the door. Pang rose up on his elbows.

"When can he leave?" Vin asked.

"Maybe never, old boy. Probably hang the sumbitch."

"They bury his father tomorrow. He has a right to mourn."

The deputy grabbed Vin's arm and pulled him out of the cell, then slammed the door shut behind him.

"He'll have to mourn there on that cot. Besides, he's not going nowheres till the sheriff gets back. Now, you go on and git outta here."

Vin turned, looked solemnly at Pang, and gave him a nod. The deputy locked the door then pushed Vin away.

As the deputy walked away, Pang realized his dilemma. His impulsive behavior had landed him in this position. He should have never gone to the saloon. If only he had stayed with his father, he would be with him now to pay his last respects and then go off on a well-planned mission to not only find justice, but save what was left of his family.

Hopefully it was not too late.

A wedge of light was cast through the small, iron-barred window, and it soon vanished with the setting sun. Pang lay sore and uncomfortable on the cot, in a quiet darkness save for the sound of cicadas outside and the hint of light from the oil lamp on the sheriff's desk. He was sure the deputy sat there, probably sleeping, or cleaning his gun, or playing solitaire.

Though Sheriff Dutton might not seem to be on his side, he likely had saved Pang's life by stopping him when he did. It was only when he was gone that the deputies reconvened their battery. In public the sheriff wouldn't have wanted to display any sort of affection toward the Chinese because it would mean political ruin. Pang's father had taught his son this reasoning of the whites. What Pang couldn't understand was how a man could follow any direction but that powered by his own heart. Maybe such ill reasoning was required to live among the people of this culture. He couldn't be certain. There were too many things about the whites that he couldn't understand.

Though rising from the cot was painful, Pang was feeling stiff and cramped and needed to stand. He made his way to his feet and shuffled slowly across the stone floor to the steel-barred window, where he could now see a crescent moon. It wasn't much to look at, but Pang envied its freedom, especially to see over all the earth, and he wished he could look down on the lives of his sister and his fiancée.

Trying to regain his health, he exercised his breathing and stretched his muscles by squatting and leaning from side to side.

He'd been in the jail three days now, trying to be patient. There was no sign of the sheriff's return. Pang wondered if the posse would be enough to take Valdar and his men. It was hard to know such things. Regardless, Pang was dedicated to seeing justice done, whether by Dutton, him, or anyone else.

During Vin's visits, he had been bringing Pang soup and

herbal tea for nutrition. He'd asked for something to ease his pain, but Vin did not believe in the man-made medicines. "It is better to heal naturally," he'd said.

Pang heard the front door to the office creak open, and the deputy spoke. "What are you doin' here so late? I fed 'im earlier. You don't need to bring 'im nothin' else."

Then Pang recognized the voice of Vin. "But he needs this special tea to help him heal."

"What's special about it?" the deputy asked.

"It is filled with herbs, and a bit of opium to help ease his pain."

*Opium?* Pang thought. *What has gotten into the old man?*

"Let me see," the deputy said.

Pang walked over to the jail door and watched the deputy lift the porcelain lid off the teapot and sniff. He made a sour face.

"That smells like hot horse piss! You gonna make 'im drink it?"

"Yes, he will drink it."

"Well—hell now, this I gotta see."

The deputy grabbed the keys off the hook on the wall, then walked over to the jail door and unlocked it. He stepped away and waved a hand for Vin to enter.

Vin stepped in front of him and winked at Pang, then turned back around and looked at the deputy.

"Well?" the deputy said. "Get on with it."

"Vin took the lid off the teapot, grabbed the handle, then swiftly emptied the contents into the deputy's face.

The deputy staggered away and dropped the keys, his eyes closed, mouth open, coughing, gagging.

Before the deputy could open his eyes, Vin stood on one

leg and like a perfectly balanced bird kicked him in the ribs. The young lawman gasped and fell backward, then lay on his side and wheezed. Vin squatted beside him and with an extended hand jabbed the back of his head.

The deputy went out cold.

Vin turned around to an astounded Pang.

"What are you doing, old man?"

"Saving your life. It's hard to say if or when the sheriff will be back, and word has gotten to us that a plan is in the works to kill you. Make it look like you were trying to escape, and then they would shoot you."

Pang looked down at the unconscious deputy, still in awe. "So what do I do now?"

"You have to go away, Pang. Do what you will with your life, but there is no more life for you here."

It was freedom he wanted, but now that he stood with it in his hands, he didn't know what to do with it. He knew he needed to go after Valdar, but he wasn't sure how, and this time he needed a plan. "I suppose you are right. I must go."

"I've been wrong many times, but I have been right more. So you go now; there is no more time for talk."

Pang bowed to his elder, then proceeded to walk away, but he stopped and looked again at the deputy. "Was that really opium?"

"No, no. You know I would never succumb to such treatments."

"Then what was it?"

Vin smirked. "Just like the deputy said. It was horse piss."

Pang spared a grin, appreciating Vin's cleaver wit, but he worried about what the old man might face for helping him. He was quite certain, however, that Vin wouldn't have done it without a plan to get out of it. So he decided not to worry, that he had enough of his own trouble to worry about.

To show his respect, he offered Vin a bow. The old man returned the gesture, and then, like a prowling lion, Pang went quietly out the door and slipped into the darkness.

Pang calculated that for breaking jail, and all the other things that the sheriff and his deputy would try to pin on him, he was already a dead man, so stealing a horse would make him no worse off. The problem at hand, however, was that he had never learned to ride a horse. When he jumped up on the horse in the alley, he realized that it was not as easy as he had thought it would be. He was sure that the horse wondered who this young man was who looked, smelled, and dressed much different than the horse's owner, and who hopped up on his back and did nothing but slap him on the withers. At least Pang knew enough to use the stirrups; that much he'd learned from watching riders on the streets of Tucson, but when it came to making the horse go, or perform any other maneuver, Pang wallowed in ignorance. Even though the horse finally gave in and took off out of the alley in an imperfect trot, when they got to the street Pang did not know how to direct him. He reached forward and pulled back hard on his mane, which caused the horse to rear and throw the Chinaman to the ground. Luckily for Pang the horse just trotted a few steps away and stopped.

He walked up slowly to the animal with his hand out, palm up. "I'm sorry, Mr. Horse, for my lack of knowledge with you. But if you give me another chance, I promise I will do better next time."

The sorrel stud bent his neck back to look at the China-man, snorted, and whickered. The activity had drawn a late night pedestrian near the scene, and after assessing it long enough, he turned and ran to the saloon. Pang knew that he had no time to waste, and after petting the stud on the neck, he remounted. Several people came running from the saloon, and one of them yelled "Horse thief!"—which was all the motivation Pang needed to use what he recalled from a horse race he once saw on the outskirts of town. He took a deep breath and hollered "YAH!" causing the stud to lunge forward. Pang held on tight to the horn of the sad-dle and let the animal lead the way, past the onlookers and down the street, and before long out into the moonlit wilderness.

Pang had no idea how far he had ridden, but at least he knew he was headed in the right direction, south, where Valdar had taken his sister and his fiancée. He knew, too, that he had to be conscious of all directions, that a posse was also looking for Valdar, and that likely a new posse had formed and would be looking for him, an escaped prisoner and horse thief. It was quite an aggravation for someone who only a few days before was sitting innocently in his tent sharing a meal with his family, and who knew how that peace was broken. It angered him to realize that the men who held him in jail, and the men who would now pursue him, were referred to as peace officers, yet they did nothing to help him restore the peace. This being so, it felt inappropriate to think of them as men. Only cowards would allow such injus-tice to occur and not follow their own hearts. And if their hearts could not see what was right, and what was truly wrong, then they definitely were not sane men, but controlled by demons.

Regardless of all that bothered him, Pang kept riding. As day began to break, he could see the light's reflection on the shallow pools of the Santa Cruz. He rode to the river and dismounted to let the horse drink and rest. Rest, however, was something that Pang didn't need. He couldn't remember a time when he had had such high adrenaline, and he felt a passionate desire to keep moving, but the lather that had surfaced on the horse around the shoulder billet and bridle told him that the horse did not share his feelings.

After the horse drank, Pang decided to walk it a ways down the riverbank. He supposed that not being hasty was a good thing, as his father had taught him that many times. A sadness crept through him as he remembered an old Chinese proverb that his father once told him:

*A wise cat does not try to outrun a dog,*
*but does catlike things to avoid him.*

With such thoughts in his mind, and the spirit of his father hovering around him, Pang tried to utilize this wisdom. The riverbank was higher than his head, and he figured that it would be difficult for his pursuers to see him, but he knew, too, that they would follow his tracks. All he had to do was look at the water to realize that tracks underneath the water could not be seen as easily, so he acted like he was heading back north, then mounted the horse, went into the water, and with his hands on its neck coaxed the animal to turn back south. He rode slowly in the river for almost a mile, then exited the water on the west side and with his voice was able to get the horse to lope.

The desert sun reached a high morning plane before Pang felt the need to stop again, and when he noticed a bluff ahead it looked like a good place to hide out of sight while he rested. The horse seemed to follow the direction of the river naturally, but to get it to go any other direction was quite a task for the inexperienced rider. Pang had learned, however, that when he got frustrated and reached down to the side of the horse's head and pulled the bridle, the horse turned in that direction. Before long he realized that the reins, which to Pang at first were just strips of leather hanging from the horse's head, could be used to turn the horse in the direction that he needed to go. He was upset with himself for not figuring that out sooner, and even more so since the horse had stepped on one of the reins and broken it, making it much shorter than the other one. Regardless, Pang and the horse communicated better, and getting it to go wherever he wanted it to go was a much simpler process.

As they approached the bluff, the horse followed a wildlife trail that led behind the bluff and then between three smaller ones. Several boulders, surrounded by prickly pear, yucca, and barrel cactus, decorated the base of each bluff, and the rocks made an inviting place to hole up for a bit and rest.

Pang rode up to the boulders to dismount, and the horse suddenly whinnied and backed away. Pang tried to hold him steady but didn't know how to, and before long the horse reared. It became uncontrollable and lunged forward so quickly that Pang fell to the ground, landing on his hip. He grimaced at the pain, rolled to his side, and watched the horse gallop away—and then he heard what had spooked the horse, a rattlesnake, only about six feet away, coiling inwardly, pulling its head back to the center of the coil, and fluttering its tail from underneath.

Pang rolled to his back and tried to crawfish away. He drew his feet back and hunched to his knees, and this sudden movement seemed to alarm the snake into a fury, but rather than spring at him, as Pang had thought it would do, the snake seemed to be lifted off the ground. It squirmed uncontrollably, and as it slowed and the dust settled around it, Pang could see blood, and a straight wooden shaft with feathers on its end stuck in the snake's head. An arrow, Pang had learned, that was used by the natives of this land.

The event dumbfounded and frightened the young Chinaman. He looked around him to see who could have shot the arrow, and a silhouette of a man in a broad hat appeared at the top of the big bluff, holding a bow with another arrow laid across it. The man stepped slowly down the bluff, and Pang's limbs seemed locked and unable to move.

"You okay, *señor*?" The man's voice was somewhat youthful and friendly.

Pang could only nod as the man came closer, his bodily features and the details of his face and clothing becoming more clear.

He looked similar to a lot of Mexicans that Pang had seen in Tucson, with a wide straw sombrero and a serape, but his skin tone was a bit lighter, and his eyes were a lighter brown. Pang had never seen a Mexican who carried a quiver and bow. Under his serape he wore lightweight trousers, home-made and not the kind sold in the town mercantile. His boots, however, were leather, with cobbled soles and square toes, just like those sold by the street merchants.

As for this man's age, Pang figured him to be in his late teens or early twenties, about his own age, with a hint of a black mustache in the early stages of growth. Besides the uniqueness of a quiver and bow, this man also wore a string of stone beads around his neck, with a wooden cross at the end, all tucked under the leather strap of the quiver that ran from the top of one shoulder to underneath the opposite arm.

"I saw you come into the bluff," the young man said as he cautiously inspected the snake, then removed the arrow nocked in his bow and put it back in the quiver. "You will not have to worry about that rattler anymore."

He reached under his pant leg and removed a knife from a sheath attached to his boot. He picked up the snake by the arrow and laid it out on one of the boulders. Pang rose slowly to his feet and watched in awe as the man removed the arrow, placed it back in his quiver, then began to cut open the snake from head to tail.

"You ever eat rattlesnake?"

Pang shook his head as he watched the man lay the knife flat and slice the skin away from the snake.

"I tried it once," the young man said, "and decided there are too many other good things to eat. But Father Gaeta likes it, so I will take it back to him. The skin I will tan and use to make something someday."

The young man folded the skin and put it in a pouch in his quiver, then cut off the tail of the snake and handed it to Pang. Pang accepted it slowly.

"Keep it. It will remind you of the dangers of the desert."

The young man then cut off the head of the snake and threw it into the rocks; then he turned to Pang and grinned. "We'll leave that for the flies and ants. Nature must always get its share of the kill. Like Father Gaeta says, even nature has its tithes."

Pang was not quite sure what to think of this man, but fear was something that he did not feel. If anything, he felt safe, but in a peculiar way—one that only human instincts could allow.

The young man wiped both sides of his knife on his pant leg, then put it back in the boot sheath. "So what is a Chinaman doing out in the dessert alone?"

Pang was afraid to answer, to give too much away, not knowing enough about this man.

The young man looked at Pang intently. "When I first saw you, I could tell that the horse you rode was not your own. That is one thing that I've learned about men who have horses. When they are riding their horse, together they are like one person. That was not the case with you."

Pang began to worry about how much this man actually knew about him, but still he was too taken by the moment to know what to say or do.

"Well," the man said, "so long as you are not a bad man, you are welcome at the mission. I know enough about Tucson to know how the Chinese are treated there. You are from Tucson, aren't you?"

Pang nodded.

"I am Enrique Osorio. I live at a mission south of here. But not for long. I'm preparing for a trip to El Paso. Do you have a name, *amigo*?"

Enrique stared at the Chinaman, waiting for an answer, and Pang thought it best to tell him. "Pang Lo."

Enrique smiled. "*Bueno*. Seen a lot of Chinamen in Tucson, but you're the first one I've ever met. Kind of funny to do so way out here in the desert."

Enrique coiled up the skinned snake meat and held it in his hand as he turned and walked away. After a few steps he stopped, turned, and looked back at the Chinaman. "You going to stay here? I'm afraid the horse you were riding is making its way back to the city, and it's a long walk back."

"I can't go back there."

"Well then, why don't you come with me?" Enrique held up the snake meat. "Father Gaeta will likely make a rattle-snake stew, and you can join us for supper."

Though the snake meat was not inviting at all, Pang knew that there was nothing more he could do but to give himself a chance to know this young man called Enrique. He felt sure that if the man had wanted to kill him, he would have done it already or, more simply, would have let the snake do it for him.

# CHAS
# DUTTON

The sheriff and his posse tracked Valdar southeast from the cottonwood where they found the gambler hanging dead. The silence that came upon them after seeing the man hanging there—a man normally impeccably dressed with a rosy complexion and abiding smile, hanging nude and pale, his flesh battered and bloody, intestines pulled from a single slice in his stomach and hanging to the ground, and flies buzzing all around—left a lasting, surreal, and chilly air. It was so wildly vile that three of the posse members deserted the search. Dutton wanted to chastise them, but the problem was that he understood. It was a lot, too, for this simple man, formerly known to most as a hardworking cowhand whose ability to handle anything from rustlers to Indians, and reputation for dealing with them in a fair and honest manner, earned him the majority vote for the office of Pima County sheriff. He was a big man, six-foot-three, with broad shoulders and a barrel chest. His eyes were a dusty green that peered out over a long and narrow nose and a bushy brown mustache that made his nostrils almost impossible to see. He was a congenial man, especially to children and elderly women, but to most men he was also bold and pragmatic, which was the only way he knew to sort the strong from the weak.

Most of his duties involved serving warrants and subpoenas and conducting an occasional theft or shooting investigation, but never anything overly dramatic. Most of the unnecessary excitement he experienced came when whiskey was involved, but in this case, with Valdar, the trouble had nothing to do with drunkenness. This was utter evil.

Valdar was the most notorious criminal known in the territory, and even the famous lawman Wyatt Earp, from nearby Tombstone, avoided going after him. But Dutton had heard from several sources that Earp and his deputized brothers used their positions in law enforcement for personal gain and put little effort into anything else. Such a code was not within Dutton's ways. He despised nepotism, and even though it was something he could not safely reveal, he despised racism as much.

He was upset with himself for not handling the situation with the Chinaman differently, but he was a law officer, and there was no law to help the Chinese. In fact it was an unwritten law in most communities led by anti-Chinese groups that to help them would be social and political suicide. Though that was wrong—and he felt it in his gut—his job was to enforce the law established by the people and not bend it. But now, with Valdar having killed the gambler, Dutton wasn't the only white man wanting justice. There was now also the rest of the posse, and any crime against a white man would bring the bounty hunters out in droves. This was the reality that Dutton would have to face, ranged against a criminal who usually committed his atrocious acts only against Mexican and Indian villages, which, at the very least, were socially out of the sheriff's jurisdiction. Because he had never interacted with or investigated him before, Valdar was pretty much a legend to Dutton. But ever since that Chinaman had come into the saloon, the legend had quickly come to life.

One thing Dutton was grateful for was the information that the Chinaman gave him. If someone had come to him with only a report of the gambler's murder, then he would not have known that Valdar had women. Because he did know it, he was certain that Valdar was on his way to Mexico to trade, which made sense judging by the direction of the tracks they followed toward the Dragoon Mountains, north of Tombstone. This direction meant only one thing to Dutton, which was that Valdar and his bandit sidekicks, with the women, were headed for El Paso, where just across the border were the people he would see for his trade.

As the mountain range became clearer, and the posse reached a higher elevation, they could see for miles behind them.

One of the posse members named Jackson loped forward to Dutton. "Riders comin', Sheriff."

Dutton stopped his horse, and the rest of the posse stopped theirs, and they looked down across the desert plain, at the band of some twenty riders who headed straight toward them, a large cloud of dust trailing behind the band.

"Who do you reckon it is?" Jackson said.

Dutton pulled a brass telescope out of his saddlebag and peered off toward the riders.

"It's Deputy Bain," Dutton said.

"Bain? What's he doin'?"

Dutton pushed the telescope closed and stuffed it back in the bag. "I don't know, but they seem to be in a hurry. Jackson, you come with me. The rest of you hold up here for a bit."

Dutton and Jackson rode down the slope to meet Bain and the other riders. The large band slowed as they approached, and the dust cloud spread and rose all around them.

"Our prisoner escaped, Sheriff," Deputy Bain said.

"Prisoner?"

"The Chinaman, sir. They threw piss in my face and—"

"You left your post and formed this posse to go after one harmless Chinaman?"

"But, sir—"

"Bain, I want you to head back to town, right now! You forget about that Chinaman and sit tight in that jail until I get back, you hear?"

"Yes, sir."

"The rest of you, join up with us if you want. We have a vicious murderer to apprehend."


It was almost dark when Enrique rode into the mission on his donkey, riding double with the Chinaman. Enrique hadn't gotten much out of him on the trip. In fact, Enrique had done most of the talking. It wasn't that he blabbed about this and that as though he had the gift of gab, but more that he was trying to get the Chinaman to respond relative to what he was saying. He was sure that Pang was in some kind of trouble, but all he really wanted to know was if he appeared to be at fault, or if it was like most cases with the Chinese, that he was facing a typical act of discrimination.

"I was born and raised in this land," Enrique had said. "My mother was born in Hermosillo and had twelve brothers and sisters. Her father brought her family to Nogales after the Mexican War, and they had a *rancho* there. Have you ever been to a real *rancho*?"

"No," Pang said.

"My grandfather was the son of a Spaniard, and all their lives they had worked as *vaqueros*. One day a handsome young Tohono O'odham Indian came to my grandfather's ranch to trade for beef, and my mother said that she fell in love with him instantly. So I am a half-breed, but for some reason my grandfather always called me a *Criollo*. I never asked him why. Do you know your family history?"

"Some of it," Pang said.

But the Chinaman didn't elaborate as Enrique had wanted him to; therefore the trip back to the mission was mostly a one-sided conversation.

The priest didn't say much as the two men dismounted from the donkey, and after Enrique introduced the Chinaman to him, all he said was "Welcome," but he did look on with a questioning, curious stare.

Enrique showed Father Gaeta the snake skin, but the priest's eyes grew wider when he showed him the meat.

"Ah, I was wondering what I'd make for supper!" the priest said.

Enrique grinned as he stuffed the meat back into the

cotton sack and tossed it to the priest. "Enjoy your feast, Father. I will be content with a jerky meal tonight."

"How about you, Pang?" the priest said. "Would you care for some of my scrumptious rattlesnake stew?"

"No, thank you. I am not hungry."

Pang's response softened the mood, and Enrique thought it best to unpack from his hunt and prepare for supper.

"Well then," the priest said, "anyway, I do hope you'll make yourself at home."

Enrique knew that the priest carried on like he wasn't concerned because that was his way; they both knew that the only reason a Chinaman would come in out of the desert was because he was in trouble. It was the level of his trouble that neither of them knew.

Pang sat at the entrance of the mission while the father prepared the stew and Enrique took the donkey to the stable. The Chinaman was still sitting there when Enrique came in with his saddlebags drooped over his shoulder and his sombrero hanging loose on his back from the thong around his neck. He coaxed the Chinaman inside and to sit at the wooden table where Enrique had eaten most of his indoor meals for the last seven years. He removed his serape and hung his sombrero on a peg near his bed. He walked up to a washbowl and rolled up the sleeves of his white cotton shirt. After washing his face and hands, he dried them on a towel then sat across from Pang at the table, poured him some milk from a stone pitcher, and cut some bread from a loaf and spread honey butter over it with the same knife.

He held the thick bread slice out in front of Pang. "You sure you're not hungry, *amigo*?"

The Chinaman merely shook his head, and then glanced

nervously at the priest, who sat down next to him with a tin plate of steaming stew.

Enrique wrinkled his nose, then bit off a chunk of his bread and chewed. "The priest eating the serpent . . . must be another of his ways of ridding the earth of sin."

Father Gaeta chuckled, and Enrique winked at the Chinaman. It was the first he had seen Pang smile, even though it was a slight smile and lasted only a few seconds. Then he was back to his uneasy demeanor, sitting away from the table on the chair, his hands in his lap and his shoulders somewhat stooped.

"So, Pang, what brings you to the desert?" the priest asked, after swallowing a bite of his stew.

The question didn't seem to be hard for the priest to ask so directly, as he took another bite of stew and awaited an answer from the Chinaman. The question certainly cut to the quick, especially since Enrique had been unable to get such an answer through his own roundabout and less direct methods.

"I am looking for someone," Pang said.

The priest nodded as he chewed, then swallowed. "And who might that be?"

"A man named Valdar. He killed my father."

Enrique felt as though he had just been jabbed in the stomach with a red-hot poker. It was the first he'd heard Valdar's name spoken in years, even though he had thought of him daily since the great tragedy of his family.

The priest had just put food in his mouth, but he stopped chewing for a moment as he looked at Enrique, then swallowed the food whole and wiped his mouth with his fingers. "Valdar . . . I see. When did this happen, my son?"

Pang looked at the priest. "A few days ago. He and two men came to our home. They took my sister and my fiancée, then killed my father. The law will not help me, so I will help myself."

Enrique quickly rose from the table and went outside the mission. He ran to the river and stopped abruptly, breathing heavily. He looked west at the orange-and-purple sunset. He had never in his life felt so frightened and exhilarated all at the same time. He thought back to the day, almost a year ago, when he and the priest had returned from a trip to Tucson, and on the way back had argued about whether or not he was ready to go to El Paso to try and find his grandfather and sister Amelia. To settle the argument, the two of them sat down across from each other at the table. They both rolled up their sleeves, put their right elbows on the table and joined hands. They stared at each other, and after the priest counted to three, the challenge began.

Enrique had never beaten the priest at arm wrestling, and they had made an agreement that he couldn't leave the mission to start his journey until he received a sign. Enrique knew the priest would never let him win intentionally, that he wanted too badly for him to forget about Valdar and start a new life with a new direction. To "turn the other cheek," he had said. But Enrique could never forgive, and never forget, no matter how hard the priest tried to get through to him with his biblical teachings.

When they were in Tucson, Enrique and the priest were drawn into a noisy alley where a crowd had gathered. A table had been set up and an arm wrestling competition was taking place. What was so ironic was that a very slender man, built similarly to the priest, had taken on a tall, stocky man, twice his size. But the slender man won in a very short time. He collected his winnings, and as he walked away, Enrique stopped him.

"How did you do that?"

The man grinned slyly and spoke with an Irish accent. "Arm wrestlin' is not a brutish sport, young lad." He pointed at his temple with his index finger. "It's all up here. You look the other feller in the eyes and you never look away. All at the same time you think yourself to the win."

Enrique looked back at the priest, who wrinkled his mouth, then said, "Rubbish."

When they returned to the mission, Enrique had not forgotten what the Irishman had told him. He concentrated hard on winning and nothing else, staring into the priest's eyes and watching the sweat beads form on his forehead, his teeth ultimately gritting. It was the priest who looked away, and down at their fists, as Enrique's arm became the dominant one. After they'd gone more than three-fourths the way down, their fists slammed on the table.

The priest looked back up at him with a gasp, but nothing was said. He looked away slowly, stood up and walked outside to the garden.

For a year they had planned for Enrique's departure, but had been waiting for the sign to go. Enrique had spent many days hunting and helping the father with the garden and saguaro fruit harvest, stockpiling food and collecting wood for the winter. He also spent time making more arrows, collecting feathers, and even made another trip to Tucson to get a new serape and a new pair of boots. In many ways he had been ready to go for months, but mentally he had never been able to put it all together. Now, he was certain, he would have to.

There was, however, one more thing that tugged at Enrique's heart. So many times the priest had asked him about accepting Christ and being baptized, but Enrique couldn't handle letting go of his anger or his desire for justice, and that was something, the priest advised, that would be required. The priest also warned him that the sign for his departure might not necessarily be from God, but from Satan. That Christ would never condone acts of violence, but that God's wrath on the evildoers could include Enrique's passion.

There was also another reason why Enrique had a hard time accepting Christ. He remembered how his father believed such religion to be nonsense, but how devout his mother was in the faith. His father had more respect for the old Indian shamans than he did for the priests of Christianity, and Enrique always believed that if the truth found him, he would know. After all the years that had passed, Enrique had made little sense of it all. He wasn't sure about God, but he did believe in the priest. It was the priest who'd found him and taken him in, not an old Indian shaman. Many of the challenges and purposes that the priest had taught him came to light. Especially now, having crossed paths with Pang. It was more than convincing.

As he turned from the river and looked back at the mission, this place that had been his home for seven years, he looked at the adobe structure, and up at the bell tower, still minus a bell, and at the garden, the stable, and at the creosote bush where he had first seen Sereno, his friendly shadow. All were so special to him. His comfort from a tragedy. His home.

Father Gaeta walked out the mission door, with Pang behind him. They stood and looked at Enrique. The priest, Enrique could tell, was worried and sad, but they had lived together long enough to know that this day would ultimately come, even though neither could ever be totally prepared for its arrival.

"Well, my son," the priest said, "I'm sure your mind is troubled."

"No," he said. "I know exactly what to do."

"And what will that be?"

"I would like you to baptize me, Father."

The priest stared solemnly for a moment and then walked close to Enrique. "You remember, Enrique, that baptizing is only a symbol. Christ must be truly in your heart to accept him."

"I accept him."

The priest put a hand on Enrique's cheek. "Then follow me."

They stepped into the river, to the deepest part, where it was up to their waists. Enrique stood with his side toward the priest, and Father Gaeta put one hand on the back of Enrique's head and the other on his stomach. The priest bent him backward, until his head was mostly submerged, and recited, "I baptize you in the name of the Father, the Son, and the Holy Spirit. Amen."

Father Gaeta brought Enrique back up, and he blinked from the water that dripped from his hair over his eyes. "I will let God lead me on this journey. It will not be of my own desires."

The priest smiled. "I will pray for you, my son."

# GERONIMO

The terrain changed considerably the farther the posse traveled into the mountains. It was hilly and rough with pine, oak, and juniper trees, and at night it was cold. When they made camp, they had gathered wood from dead trees fallen, and some still standing; they broke off limbs and mixed them with mesquite to make a nice, hot fire to deaden the chill. But it was more than the chill in the air that brought discomfort to Sheriff Dutton. Earlier that day, in the afternoon, they had wandered upon a military party led by General George Crook, who informed them of several Apache on the warpath, led by the Chiricahua chief Geronimo. As if it wasn't already enough to worry about a savage killer on the loose, who could ambush them at any time, now they were aware that warring Apaches could ignite just as devastating an attack on the posse. The Apaches knew the land and terrain better than anyone, while Valdar was more vile, fearless, and manipulative. But the two of them together, and both on the enemy side, was like riding inside the gates of hell.

Dutton knew that their safety improved with their numbers. With more than forty members in the posse, he was able to establish shifts of men to stand guard while others slept. Very few, however, especially Dutton, could sleep. Most of them just lay on their bedrolls watching the fire, drinking coffee with one hand, and holding their guns with the other. Little conversation took place, other than when Dutton made his rounds to check on everyone. He took particular notice of a young man named Dempsy, maybe twenty years old, who clutched a knife between his hand and coffee cup. His hand shook a bit when he took a drink, and the nickel-finished .45 Colt revolver in his other hand rested on his bent knee and reflected the firelight. Dutton noticed, too, a Winchester lever-action rifle at Dempsy's feet.

Dutton squatted beside him and shared the view of the glowing embers. "We got a long day tomorrow, so we'll rise early. You boys should try and get some sleep."

A man named Payne spoke from across the fire, his sunburned cheeks and forehead glowing above a black beard. "Hell, Sheriff, we can't sleep no easier than you can."

Dutton half-grinned and nodded. "Yeah, I reckon you're right."

Dempsy emptied his coffee cup into the fire, then dropped the cup next to him but held on to the knife. "How far away from Valdar you reckon we are, Sheriff?"

"It's hard to tell, but I'd say he's not far. He's turned back south. Will probably ride close to the Mexico border all the way to El Paso."

"What's your plan to get him?" Payne said.

"I'll know more how to do it when we find him. My hope is to surround him and just shoot them all, dead. Just try not to shoot the women."

"Ah hell," Dempsy said. "They're just China girls. I ain't taking no chances on missin' anyone. I'm gonna just open fire and kill them all."

Dutton stared at the young man gravely. "I don't care what kind of girls they are, they're victims, and everyone here is to treat them as such. *Comprende?*"

Dempsy glanced embarrassingly at the others around the fire, and Dutton stood up and went back to his own bedroll. He lay down, put his hands behind his head, and gazed up at the stars. He took in a deep breath of cool air through his nose and worried about how his posse would handle this situation. It was hard enough to know he had two enemies out there, let alone worry about racially driven men who might act out of stupidity and botch the whole campaign.

It made him wish he was still a cowhand. He'd spent many nights just like this one sleeping out on the range, studying the constellations in the sky, but thinking only about a roundup in the morning, or maybe about a few Apaches stealing beeves, but never anything this worrisome. Why did he ever let them talk him in to running for sheriff? He closed his eyes and brought his hand out to rub them. "You're a damned fool, Chas Dutton."


Enrique had spent most of the evening packing, and couldn't sleep at all that night. He lay in his bed thinking about what it was going to be like trailing Valdar and how he would confront him. He really didn't care how he killed him; he just wanted to make sure Valdar saw his face when he did it, that the last vision the lunatic had in his dying eyes was that of Enrique Osorio.

Pang let it be known that he would be shouting his father's name when he delivered the last blow. When Enrique asked him how he would kill him, Pang held up his hand. How foolish, he thought, that the Chinaman believed he could kill such a man with his bare hands, and he told him so. To prove him wrong, Pang had Father Gaeta hold up a large stone crock, and not far from the priest, he had Enrique hold between his hands a thick oak board that the priest used to cut vegetables and meat. Pang stood between Enrique and the priest, with both of them no more than two arm lengths away.

Pang closed his eyes, put his hands over his chest in a praying position, took a deep breath through his nose, and then exhaled through his mouth. When his eyes opened, it was like a flash of light. Pang rose up on one leg and kicked the stone crock, shattering it into a pile of broken fragments and dust, and then pivoted on his leg, squared away in front of Enrique, and with a downward thrust of his arm, his hand elongated, he yelled and brought the hand down on the board, splitting it in half.

Enrique and the priest both stood astounded as Pang straightened back up, put his hands back together, and took another deep breath.

"Bravo," Father Gaeta said, looking over all the broken fragments. "I'm quite impressed." He placed a hand on Pang's shoulder and offered a slight smile. "But don't think

I don't expect you to replace my best water crock and cutting board, and clean up the mess."

Pang nodded, then looked at Enrique, who stood still in awe, with his mouth slightly agape.

"How'd you do that?" Enrique said.

"My father taught me."

"Can you teach me?"

"It takes many years to teach such things. I cannot do it in only a few days."

"I wouldn't worry about it, my son," the priest said to Enrique as he handed Pang a straw broom. "You are skilled at things that Pang is not. Together, with both of your skills, and of course with God's help, you will be able to realize your passions."

Enrique couldn't stop thinking about this new edge. For the past seven years he had always imagined killing Valdar by himself, or maybe with the help of his grandfather, but the thought of a Chinaman accompanying him with such a special fighting skill was beyond anything he'd ever dreamed. But it wasn't so much this new company; he saw Pang as much more than a partner in his pursuit. Now there were two men that wanted Valdar's blood, one as bad as the other, and the real challenge would be not just to kill Valdar, but to share in the glory.

Baliador held the captured Apache with a knife to his throat, and Beshkah sat nearby on a boulder, with one leg propped up on an opposite rock, twirling the rowels of one of his spurs with the tip of his pistol barrel.

Several Apache rode into camp with Geronimo centered among them. Valdar sat near the campfire chewing the meat off the rib bone of a lame horse they'd killed the day before. When he saw the Apaches, he smiled, threw the bone into the fire, and wiped his mouth on his shirtsleeve. He walked to the other side of the fire as the Apache spread out and Geronimo worked his way to the front on a dappled gray, bald-faced horse.

Valdar looked around him and quickly knew he was surrounded, but he was certain that the Apache wouldn't attack and risk losing their fellow brave.

"I take it that we have something you want," Valdar said to the chief, in a Spanish dialect he knew he'd understand.

"You are the Demon Warrior who raids the camps of the Tohono O'odham and steals their women. We have no fight with you."

Valdar sucked his teeth then spat into the fire. "No, *señor*, I am not a fighter, I am more like the Antichrist."

Beshkah and Baliador laughed.

Geronimo found no humor in Valdar's words and only looked at him sternly.

Valdar pointed with his thumb back at the captured Apache. "What do you have in trade?"

"Protection."

Valdar laughed mockingly. "What do we need protection from, *señor*? From you crazy Chiricahuas?"

"We know that the white man has rewards for your heads. There are more than forty riders that camped last night and are now coming this way. You give us back my nephew, and I will make sure the riders never find you."

Valdar had a more serious look about his face. "What makes you think the riders are after us?"

"A white man was found gutted and hanging in a tree. If they thought the Apache did it, then only the bluecoats would be out riding. Those men are a white man's posse."

It did not take Valdar long to ponder the offer. He nodded to Baliador, who brought the Apache forward. Valdar took ahold of the hostage himself.

"Call your men away," the bandit said. "We will take this nephew of yours and turn him loose in the mountains, then we have our deal."

Geronimo contemplated Valdar's words. "How do we know you will do as you say?"

"Ah, you don't, *señor*. But I know you like to gamble, and we both stand too much to lose in this game."

The chief looked around at his men and motioned them in. Valdar watched, and a smile formed on his face.

"*Muy bien*," he said.

Geronimo turned, as did the rest of his band, and dust kicked up behind them as they rode south into the desert wilderness.

Baliador and Beshkah grabbed the women, who now numbered three. Along with Sai Min and Mun Lo, they had captured a half-breed Tohono O'odham girl with light brown eyes and auburn hair, a sure sale to the Mexican *patrón* across the river from El Paso. They tied the women one behind the other and behind the Apache, then had them walk in a line as their captors rode horses in front of them.

When they reached a steep canyon in the mountains, Valdar had Beshkah ride to the top to look out. When he motioned that it was clear, Baliador cut loose the Apache and pushed him to the ground. The timid man lay there with his hands still tied and watched them ride away with the women.

The Apache had meant nothing to Valdar, but he was amazed at how valuable he had become. Beshkah's own Apache instincts had helped him catch the Indian while he spied on their camp. Valdar had had no idea what they would do with him. He had contemplated letting Beshkah and Baliador use him for target practice with their knives, but when they noticed more Apache coming into their camp, in a number that would easily overwhelm them, he knew the young Indian would be a possible negotiation piece.

Now he only hoped that the Apache kept their end of the bargain, but he took no chances. He put each of the women on the horses behind him and his two *compadres*, and they rode around the forest of Pedregosa and toward the territory of New Mexico.

The scout that Dutton had sent on ahead of the posse rode back toward them in a hurry. It forced Dutton to look around him for signs of trouble, but he saw none; then all of the sudden the scout's horse reared and the man fell off into a cloud of dust. Dutton had the men divide up and hold back as he and Jackson rode toward the fallen rider. Fear tugged at his nerves when they arrived to find the scout dead with an arrow in his back.

Dutton dismounted quickly, as did Jackson, both drawing their guns, squatting and looking over the backs of their horses.

"Where are they, Sheriff?" Jackson said.

"How the hell am I supposed to know? They're Apaches."

"But you've fought them before. You know what they do."

"All I know is that they're damned sneaky, and with the army after them, they'll be full of fire."

Dutton waved his gun at the rest of the posse, motioning both groups to go into cover. The riders spread out, heading for the rocks, but that's when they came, fifty or sixty Apache, Dutton calculated, on horseback and chanting a war cry.

"Ah hell," Dutton said, holstering his .45 revolver and pulling his horse into the rocks. He pulled his rifle from its scabbard, rested his arm over a boulder, and began firing. It was such a dusty frenzy that he hardly knew where to shoot, in fear of hitting his own men, so he held back and didn't fire. What was strange to the sheriff, however, was how the Apache didn't seem to be fighting, but more like chasing. Seldom did an Apache shoot his rifle, and when he did, it was in the air or to shoot back. Besides the scout killed with the arrow, neither side was losing men, so it wasn't a bloodbath. The worst of it was that Dutton's posse was divided and scattering among the foothills, and it would be difficult for them to defend themselves should a proper attack occur.

Dutton motioned to Jackson, who hid behind a rock, shooting his revolver aimlessly. Jackson stopped firing, and the Apache were soon riding away, their chants becoming a distant and fading cry.

Dutton remounted his horse and rode out into the open, and Jackson soon joined him.

"What was that all about?" Jackson said.

"Hell if I know," Dutton said, looking over at the dead body of his scout. "All I know is that they didn't come for a fight as much as they did just to mess us up. If they wanted a battle with us, they'd have been relentless."

"So why'd they do it?"

Dutton looked around him. "All I can figure is that now we're spooked and scattered, which will do nothing but slow us down."

"You don't think they're working for Valdar, do you?"

"It's hard to tell. But it's the only thing I can make sense of."

Dutton and Jackson rode along the foothills assessing the situation, finding only one dead Apache, one leg-shot horse, and the blood trail of others. Then they found three of the posse, dead. All Dutton could do was tip his hat back and shake his head. How senseless and out of whack everything seemed. A manhunt was never easy, but this was unlike anything Dutton had ever experienced. Typically an outlaw was chased down, and if he was found, a shootout would occur, and eventually one or the other side surrendered. But this was more than a showdown. This was evil mind games.

An hour passed before he could gather all the men up again. Some wouldn't even come out of hiding, and several banded up and headed back toward Tucson. There were twenty-two men left in the posse, and one wounded, Dempsy, who had taken a bullet in his shoulder.

They built a fire and laid him next to it, while Jackson heated a knife. It took five men to hold the young man down while Jackson dug out the bullet and cauterized the wound. They gave Dempsy a bottle of whiskey while they bandaged him up.

Dutton looked on. "Jackson, I'll need you as a scout now.

Ride ahead and see if you can pick up Valdar's trail again. Payne, you help Dempsy back on his horse and take him back to Tucson. The rest of you help me bury the dead."

"That just leaves us with twenty men, Sheriff," Jackson said.

"I know. I can count."

"But what if we're attacked again, the men can't stand against that many Apaches."

"Those Apaches won't be back. They've headed toward Mexico, where they're hiding from the army. We're going straight east, where Valdar is headed. And we'll have to travel pretty fast to catch up to him."

Jackson sighed and headed to his horse, and within two hours Payne and Dempsy were on their way back home. Within the same amount of time the dead were buried and the dwindled posse was once again on the trail of Valdar. Though his job as sheriff was not the worst job he'd ever had, Dutton felt now that it was more than he'd ever bargained for. Sure, there were risks, as were to be expected. But the odds on this assignment were terribly risky for all involved. Dutton prayed for a better way, because this one was not working.

# EL PASO
# WAY

Enrique and Pang prepared two mules and a burro for their journey. The priest thought it best to equip Pang with clothing more suitable to the desert, so Enrique gave him one of his extra serapes and, since the Chinaman had smaller feet, a pair of his older boots that he'd outgrown. For a hat they gave him a gringo's hat, a derby, that the priest had found on a trail and brought back to the mission. It was faded brown from lying under the desert sun, but it fit and seemed more appropriate than the Chinaman's own cap.

Pang wore the attire reluctantly, but for some reason he thought it might be a good idea to disguise himself a bit, since people would be looking for him. He even tucked his queue under the back of the serape, which, aside his personal attire, was the next most recognizable symbol of his race.

The mules they would ride, but on the burro they packed most of the food and camping supplies. Their bedrolls, canteens, and saddlebags, however, would be kept on their own mules. That way, Enrique assured Pang, if they were thirsty they would not have to stop to drink. And if they were separated from the burro, they would still have water and some jerky to eat.

Enrique filled his quiver with more arrows and feathers and sinew than he'd ever carried before. He would not have time to make new ones, nor would he worry about looking for any that went astray. This was a journey where time was critical, and the essence was not survival, but justice.

Pang mounted his mule, and Enrique checked the cinch and bridle on his own. The priest walked up to him and helped with the cinch. Enrique tried not to look at him, but when it came time to mount, he knew he had to.

The priest smiled, as he usually did, showing his teeth among the thick brown beard, but this time the smile vanished quickly and tears formed in his eyes. He grabbed Enrique and embraced him tightly. Enrique closed his eyes and tried to hold back the emotion that swelled inside him.

The priest let go and looked back at Enrique. "God be with you, my son."

Enrique looked away timidly, then quickly let go of the priest and mounted his mule. He turned to Pang and nodded, and they both nudged their mules and headed them due east, with the burro in tow behind Enrique. He thought of looking back, but knew it was best not to. It was time to look ahead and face his destiny, with hope he would find justice, and that one day he would see the priest again.


From the east bank of the Santa Cruz, Enrique and Pang rode along the foothills of the piñon-studded Santa Rita

Mountains. Enrique was quite concerned about Sereno, who, by the time they reached the Canelo Hills that night, was still following them. He surely wouldn't follow them all the way to El Paso. The next morning, however, he was still there, just fifty yards to their north, disappearing occasionally, only to return later.

It was on their second day, traveling on the crest of a mountain in the Huachuca range, when Pang first saw Sereno. He stopped his mule abruptly and the mule brayed. "Did you see that?" Pang said. "Someone is following us."

"Not to worry," Enrique said. "That is only our watchman. Out little Tohono O'odham guardian angel."

Pang narrowed his eyes in confusion.

"Come on, let's keep riding," Enrique said, "and I'll tell you about him."

During the story, Pang kept lagging a little behind and gawking to their left, looking for signs of the Tohono O'odham orphan again, but rarely seeing him.

"Don't worry," Enrique said. "Sereno is our friend, and he will come through for us when no one else will."

That night they camped in an arroyo and by a stream, where they refilled their canteens and cooked a rabbit over an open fire. The rabbit Enrique had shot late in the afternoon along the trail. He'd stopped his mule, gotten down, and crept along the edge of mountain draw where he'd seen a rabbit run behind a cluster of gnarly junipers. He hunched low, pulled his bow from its sleeve and a short arrow from the quiver, never taking his eyes off the rabbit, then drew and released the arrow. He went after his kill and came out from behind the juniper with the evening supper.

He explained to Pang that hunting daily would be a sure

way of saving the jerky, bread, and dried fruits they'd brought along from the mission. There would be emergency days—such as during heavy rains, or on Valdar's trail, which they wouldn't want to leave—when there would be no time for hunting. The food they packed would be used as emergency rations. But on any other day, they would eat from a fresh kill.

The first night at camp was mostly a quiet night, with very little conversation. Pang sat hunched up by the fire, often glancing in the direction of sounds from nocturnal wildlife. Enrique explained them all to him, the rodents and their footsteps, the hoot of the owl, the howl of the coyote, but Pang seemed no more at ease. On their second night, Enrique decided to help occupy Pang's mind with conversation, in hope of minimizing his discomfort.

Enrique wanted to know more about what happened to Pang's father, but he understood the delicateness of such matters. He thought the only way to know would be to tell Pang his own story, but all the Chinaman would do was stare at the fire and occasionally nod. The gory details seemed to get a little more of his attention, but Enrique sensed that he was uncomfortable hearing the story, so he changed the subject.

"I am very intrigued by your abilities," he said.

"What abilities?" Pang answered.

"How you broke the crock, and the board. I would have broken my foot and hand. How did you do that?"

"It's no different than your ability to shoot your arrows. I couldn't do that either. But for many years we have learned these talents and with much practice have mastered the abilities."

Enrique nodded, reached to the fire, and turned the rabbit as it roasted on a skewer.

"Do you think you could teach me?" Enrique said.

They looked at each other, and Pang shrugged. "I could try, but it will take time."

"I understand, but I am a fast learner. In trade I will teach you to shoot the bow and arrow."

Pang nodded. "What you want to learn is called kung fu. My father was my teacher, and when I was little he always told me that the body cannot act until the mind is first clear. That was the first lesson."

"It seems like a wise statement, but how do you use it?"

Pang rose to his knees then sat back on his heels, and he instructed Enrique to do the same. The *Criollo* followed his instruction, and Pang started breathing deeply, with his eyes closed. After three deep breaths, he opened his eyes and looked at Enrique.

"The brain works best when the blood that flows through it is rich with oxygen. Daily, when we meditate, we breathe, in through the nose, out the mouth, in heavy breaths. And if a need for defense ever arises, it's like second nature to take a heavy breath so the mind will help you in your defense."

Enrique copied Pang and breathed deeply several times, feeling the pleasure to his lungs and the relaxation of his body. He smiled and looked at Pang. "I like this. What is next?"

"One does not learn kung fu in one night. You must master the first two lessons first, then I will give you lesson three."

Enrique thought about both lessons, and caught himself

doing the breathing exercises and thinking in a preoccupied fashion about busting the crock.

When the rabbit was cooked, Enrique tore off a leg and handed it to Pang. The Chinaman took it reluctantly and bit into it carefully, but he eventually nodded his approval to the cook. Enrique then wrapped another leg of the rabbit in a cloth, along with some bread, and took it north into the darkness and sat it on a boulder. He placed another rock on top of it, a system that he and Sereno were both familiar with.

After they ate, Enrique threw his bones into the fire and went to the stream to wash his hands and face. When he returned, Pang was cuddled up under his bedroll, his eyes still open, the embers of the fire glowing on his face and reflecting in his eyes.

"In the morning I will give you your first arrow lesson," Enrique said.

Pang nodded, then closed his eyes, and Enrique sat back down and practiced his breathing until his own eyes felt heavy and sleep consumed them both.

Whenever Enrique camped in the desert, he was used to waking to the social calls of many birds, but this morning the land around the Huachuca was particularly quiet. Because of this change of nature, his awakening was peculiarly uneasy. He looked up into the coral sky to the east, and the only normal sense was the smell of the smoldering coals of the fire. When his eyes had completely focused, the first thing he noticed was that Pang was gone, as was his bedroll. Enrique walked quickly about, looking in all directions, and that's when he saw Pang sitting on the crest of a bluff, facing the eastern sky. He was sitting the way he had when he demonstrated the breathing technique to Enrique. His posture was straight and his hands were uniform in his lap. He steadily rose to his feet, raised his hands, bent, and touched the ground, then stood in a sprawling stance, jumped, and kicked, all the while holding his hands out in front of him.

Enrique wasn't sure what the Chinaman was doing, but he decided that it wasn't good to worry, and went about stoking the fire and rolling up his own bedroll. After tying it on the mule, he went up to the boulder where he'd left the piece of rabbit the night before and found the rock back on top of the cloth, with the contents gone. The system had once again proven itself. With the rock back on top, Enrique was confident that Sereno had gotten the food instead of a desert varmint.

Enrique squatted next to the fire, warmed his hands, and was finishing his morning prayer when Pang walked back into the camp.

"What were you doing up there?" Enrique asked.

"Lessons one and two," Pang said.

"I don't remember kicking being part of those lessons."

"That is because I did not teach you all of the lesson. Breathing is the beginning. Then the muscles must be stretched, and the blood must circulate well to feed those muscles."

Enrique was beginning to get frustrated with the China-man, but he decided not to let it bother him. He stood and kicked at the fire, spreading the coals apart. "We better get riding."

They put the blankets on their mules, tied on the pack

burro, and proceeded east into a mountain draw. After riding a mile Enrique heard the unique whistle, as if a bird and mammal had joined voices, and saw Sereno dash away into hiding. This, Enrique knew, was an alert not just of something near, but of possible danger. That's when several men on horseback began to appear on a ridge south and east of them. He stopped his mule abruptly. "Whoa!"

Pang followed suit and made his confusion apparent as he gawked aimlessly.

The men on the ridge, at least twenty Enrique counted, stood on their horses and stared at them.

"Who are they?" Pang said.

"Apache, for sure," Enrique said. "We just don't know how friendly."

Enrique had learned enough about the Apache to know that it was always better to go on about your business than to ever appear frightened or aggressive. He also knew that the enemy to the Apache at this time was not the Mexicans, the Tohono O'odham, or even other warring Indian tribes, but the white man. What he did not know was how they felt about Chinamen.

He decided to keep riding and nudged his mule forward. Pang followed him.

"What do we do?" Pang said.

"We go about our business. Look at them occasionally. Let them know that we see them. If they are worried about us, then they will surround us. If not, they'll just likely watch us ride on."

The two rode for another mile through the lengthy draw, and several of the Apache disappeared; only two remained on the ridge. Enrique began to wonder if they were surrounding them, and then he saw a large group riding toward them.

"Keep riding," he told the Chinaman. "Don't let them think you're afraid."

"But I am afraid," Pang said.

"Well, let that be lesson number one from me in dealing with Apache. Never show them your fear."

Enrique was not as concerned until he saw other riders appear to their north as well, and then when he turned and looked behind them he saw more. He was sure now that whatever the Apache wanted, they'd likely get it.

When the riders ahead of them were within fifty yards, Enrique and Pang stopped their mules. The Apache got closer and spread out in front of them and behind them, and several loped their horses up the slope of the mountain base on each side of them, and all eventually stopped. They were like most Apache Enrique had seen before. Cloth headbands around their foreheads; long, silky black hair; deerskin leggings or loincloths; and moccasins. They all carried rifles. Their horses were a variety of colors—many paints, sorrels, and bays—but one particular horse caught Enrique's attention. It was a dappled gray with a bald face and pink eyes, and it worked its way through the riders ahead of him and stopped just a few feet away. Two other riders came up from behind, and each took his place on one side of the dapple gray.

Horses snorting and whickering were the only sounds, and the seriousness on all of the Apache faces could have stopped a dust storm. What Enrique noticed most, however, was how this man on the bald-face horse kept staring at Pang. Then he looked back and forth between both Enrique and Pang and spoke in his known Spanish dialect. "Who are you people?"

Once Enrique began to speak, all eyes looked at him. "I am Enrique Osorio. I am born of this land and am a friend to the Apache. This man who rides with me is no threat to you."

The leader studied Pang again. "I have seen his kind before, many moons ago when the white man built the trails of the iron horse. But they did not wear a white man's clothes."

Enrique thought about how strange the derby and serape must look on the Chinaman. "He only wears the clothes to protect himself from desert travel."

"I am Geronimo, chief of the *Nnee*, and of the land of my people. Why do you tread on our land?"

Enrique had heard of Geronimo, and how he had fled the reservation and made war with the army. He had rarely heard, however, Apache refer to themselves as *Nnee*, which meant "the People" in their own native language. Apache was a name given to them by the Spanish, and *Nnee* was typically only used during conversations with their own people. Enrique understood this because the Spanish called his own Tohono O'odham people *Papago*, which was a name that his fellow tribesmen rejected. This meant that the Apache were fed up with the centuries of lies offered them by the Spanish, the Mexicans, and now the Americans.

"We are on the trail of Antonio Valdar. We do not pose any threat to the *Nnee*. We just want to pass through and make it to El Paso before Valdar does."

"What is this business you have with the Demon Warrior?"

Enrique was not surprised that the Apache had knowledge of Valdar, and was no more surprised at the name he had been given. "Justice, Chief. Pang and I want his blood."

There was silence for a moment, then Geronimo nodded at the men behind the *Criollo* and they held up their rifles. They came forward, and the ones on the hillside came down closer, and one of them cut loose the pack burro and pulled the braying animal away.

Enrique looked to Geronimo for an answer.

"The Demon Warrior is a friend to my people. You say you are a friend to the Apache, but we do not know you. We will take you back to our camp and hold a trial. That will decide your fate."

Pang looked around nervously as the Apache men drew closer to them. "What do we do?"

"We go with them," Enrique said.

"Maybe we should fight them."

Enrique looked at Pang with disgust. "You try anything and you'll get us both killed. There is no bow and arrow or kung fu that will outfight these men. We stand a much better chance back at their camp."

Before Enrique could say another word, he and Pang were in the clutches of the men, who tied their arms tight against their torso with leather. Pang tried to fight, but Enrique's voice calmed him to an easy surrender. "Don't fight it! It will only make things worse!"

Pang was breathing heavily, but it was not an exercise. He called out in his own Chinese tongue, in words that Enrique didn't understand, but his tone was very clear. The Chinaman was showing his anger and his fear.

*   *   *

Jackson and a man named Farrell had tracked Valdar through the Pedregosa and thought he'd probably crossed the border into the New Mexico Territory, but the trail came to a dead end. The two men studied a camp but saw no trail out.

"Where do you think they went?" Farrell said.

"I can't figure," Jackson said. "Either they turned back, or they are right on top of us."

Farrell looked around him nervously. "So what do we do now?"

"We better head back and tell the sheriff."

The two men started back, and as they passed through a steep cut in the mountains, Jackson noticed his horse's ears twitch, and on occasion it raised its head and peered to the south.

"What's the matter?" Jackson said, patting the horse on the neck.

The horse suddenly reared and Farrell fell from his own mount. Jackson pulled his horse back to find Farrell lying dead with a knife in his chest. He looked around to see where the knife might have come from, but before he could ascertain anything, his hat flew off and a rope fell around his chest and tightened. He was pulled down from his horse, and the spooked steed ran away, only to be captured by another lasso.

Jackson rolled in his own dust and to his back, and when he looked up, he stared into the grinning face of a man with a thin black mustache. The man reached down, grabbed him by the shirt placket, and picked him up to his feet. He pushed him back to his horse and laid him over its back, then tied his feet together.

The man pulled Jackson's horse to his own, which he mounted, and pulled Jackson around the bend and into the rocks, where they joined two other men and what appeared to be three women prisoners. When they stopped, the man came back and pushed Jackson off the horse and to the ground.

Another man, who smelled foul from tequila, pulled him up to a sitting position. The man laughed. "You look like you've had a rough day, *señor*." The other men followed with laughter. "So, did you find what you were looking for?"

Jackson could not answer, but he knew that he was staring into the face of one of the most evil men he'd ever heard tell of. He also knew that it was likely his life was over, but just how soon, or how quickly he would die, was the critical unknown.

"So, *amigo*, I hear there are many men looking for me, but you and your poor *compadre* back there are only two men. Are there more *hombres* you should tell me about?"

"I ain't tellin' you nothin', you sick sumbitch." Jackson spit in Valdar's face.

Valdar's fury was short-lived, as he wiped the saliva from his cheek then laughed and summoned Beshkah. The bandit came forward, his spurs jingling and the tips of his shoes glistening in the sunlight. He stood next to Valdar, and Valdar grabbed Jackson by the chin and lifted him to his feet. He forced him to a boulder and slammed him against it.

"This man is complaining about his knees," Valdar said. "Do you have something for the pain?"

Beshkah grunted and stepped in front of Jackson as Valdar backed away. In one swift motion, Beshkah reared a leg back then kicked forward, busting Jackson's knee with his steel plated shoe. The posse scout screamed in agony.

Valdar came close to his face and breathed the same stale breath as he heckled him. "How's the pain, *muchacho*? Is it better now?"

Jackson stared back at Valdar with watery eyes. "You'll rot in hell for what you do."

Valdar turned to Beshkah. "I guess it was not enough medicine. Give him some more."

Beshkah reared back and kicked the other knee, and Jackson fell to the ground screaming. Valdar hunched to the ground and leaned over in front of his face, grabbing his chin with his hand. Jackson fought for his breath as Valdar turned his face to his own.

"Now, if you think I will kill you before you tell me anything, you're badly mistaken, *señor*. You tell me what I want to know and you'll die much quicker."

Jackson didn't trust this monster in any way, but torture was something that he knew Valdar would continually subject him to until he got what he wanted. Whether he would actually kill him or not was uncertain, but at this point, with the image of the naked gambler in his mind, he figured it was worth the gamble.

"There is a posse," Jackson said in a mumble, followed by a heavy breath and a grimace.

Valdar squeezed his chin tighter. "How many?"

"Eighteen. About a mile west of here."

Valdar let go and lightly slapped Jackson's face. "Ah, now that wasn't so hard, was it, *amigo*?"

Jackson swallowed and closed his eyes, then he felt Valdar grab him by the hair and hold his head back against the boulder. Beshkah then came forward, stood before him, lifted his boot, and with a steady swipe, brought the rowel of his spur across Jackson's neck. There was only a slight sting at first, but then he realized he could not breathe, and felt the warm blood flowing down his neck and onto his chest. To Jackson's recollection, this was the only time he'd ever gambled and won.

Enrique and Pang sat back to back, their wrists tied together, at the trunk of a dead cottonwood. The Apache camp was not like those Enrique had seen before, with grass wickiups but less primitive, with makeshift shelters of poles, deerskin, and the white man's canvas. It was, indeed, a camp for a tribe constantly on the move.

Several men sat outside near a fire, while the women prepared meals and the children played. But a majority of the men were inside one of the shelters, deciding the fate of their two captives.

Enrique felt bad for Pang, knowing that after all he had recently gone through, this moment only added to his pain.

"I'm sorry," Enrique said.

"For what?" Pang answered, as he squirmed and rolled his wrists.

"For getting you into this mess. I know it was not in your plan."

"I'm sure it was not in your plan, either. I do not blame you."

Enrique could tell that the Chinaman's words were genuine. "And I was supposed to teach you how to shoot the bow today."

Pang sighed and pulled his wrists free. "Such a lesson is the least of my worries," he said, now looking at Enrique and untying him.

"How did you get free?" Enrique said, looking at the Chinaman, dumbfounded.

"Apache might be good at surrounding and capturing, but they are not good at tying knots."

Enrique rubbed his arms where the leather ties had cut into them and made them sore. He decided not to question Pang's tactics and, like him, to take advantage of their new freedom. "I'm not sure where they've taken our mules . . . They must be tied on the other side of the shelters."

"We must find them, and quickly," Pang said, "without alarming the women and children."

At that moment at least twenty Apache rode into the camp. Their women chanted as they dismounted, and Geronimo and the other men came out of their shelters to greet them. There was a long discussion with one of the riders, and then Geronimo looked in the direction of Enrique and Pang as they sprinted across the camp.

Several of the Apache headed them off and surrounded them. The two men stopped, looking all around as the braves closed in. Enrique was surprised at how poised Pang seemed all of the sudden, crouching, with his hands elongated in front of his face.

One of the Apache quickly lunged at Enrique. The two of them fell to the ground, muscles tight and teeth clenched as they rolled in the dust, each trying to gain control over the other. Enrique gained nothing fast, as two other braves joined in the fight and quickly subdued him. It was when they held him up, one holding each arm, that the real fight began.

Several Apache tried to subdue the Chinaman, but Pang was quick to stop them, with either a jab to the neck, a kick to the stomach, or both a punch and a kick that quickly disabled the attacker. But all stopped after a rifle was shot into the air, and every head turned to Geronimo, who stood next to several other Apache, one with a rifle pointed at Pang.

Geronimo nodded to his brave to lower the rifle and then they proceeded toward them. He looked over all of his fallen men, who stood slowly, moaning and grimacing, except one who lay unconscious.

"You kill one of my men," Geronimo said, looking sternly at Pang.

"No," Pang said, walking to the fallen brave, stooping and slapping his face lightly with the back of his hand. "He's just, like you say, taking a *siesta*."

The chief nodded and then looked at both the men. "The council has decided. You are free to go."

Enrique looked over at Pang, who rose slowly, as if not convinced of they newly granted freedom.

"May I ask how you came to your decision?" Enrique asked, looking at Geronimo.

"The Demon Warrior has betrayed us. He promised to free one of our men, but set him free only to follow him and kill him later. For this betrayal we approve of your pursuit to kill him, and the two Apache who follow him. They no longer live the *Nnee* way and are nothing to our people. To help you, I will send two of my warriors with you. But that is all I can spare."

Enrique looked at the two men—short, muscular, and youthful. "Thank you," Enrique said.

Two women came forward pulling the mules and the burro, all their belongings still intact. One of the women handed Enrique his quiver and bow. Geronimo complimented him on the weapon.

"Our council recognized your *Nnee* bow and arrow, and that the shafts were new. Only someone who knew the *Nnee* way could have made those arrows. It was agreed by the council that you were very likely a friend to the *Nnee*."

Enrique nodded then reached into one of his saddlebags and grabbed all of the jerky and dried fruits. He handed them to Geronimo.

"For you and your people. You will need food for strength during your battles. Let it be a peace offering."

Geronimo nodded and had one of the women take the goods; then he took one step toward Enrique, pulled a knife from his waist, and drew a cut on his hand.

Enrique knew what he wanted and did the same, and in the same fashion as he arm wrestled the priest, the two men joined hands, looked each other squarely in the eyes, and became blood brothers of the Sonora.


When Dutton and the posse rode up on Jackson and Farrell's bodies, the men had seen enough. All of them, except the lawman, turned and headed back. They didn't even stay to help bury the bodies, or try to talk him out of staying, and there was nothing Dutton could do to stop them. He could have cursed them as cowards, but he wasn't sure it was cowardice that made them turn back. It was likely plain old common sense. He wasn't even sure what made him stay, but he was quite certain it wasn't courage, and he was damn certain it wasn't common sense. He supposed it was duty, but also stubbornness and pride. He was not about to go to his grave backing out on something he was paid to do. It might not be a healthy job, but at least it was an honorable job. Stubborn or not, honor was something he was certain he'd be comfortable taking to the grave.

After he buried the bodies, Dutton wanted to build a fire and make some coffee, but he remembered that the camping supplies were with one of the other riders. All he had was some jerky and a sack of raisins that he always carried with him, in case he had to ride a ways out of town. He was more than a ways out of town now; he figured he was close to New Mexico Territory. With only a few hours of daylight left, he supposed it best to head up into the mountains, where Valdar likely wouldn't be, maybe shoot a deer or pronghorn, have a warm meal, and head out toward El Paso the next day with a full belly and a fresh start. Yes, that was a plan that would likely work and not take him to his grave any sooner than he wanted to go.

Enrique gave all their food away for two reasons. First, he knew it would please Geronimo and buy them lasting friendship. Plus, it would prove that he not only had the knowledge of making Apache weapons, but he could also use them. To give up his food meant he could hunt and kill for survival. Such a man would be worthy of his freedom and welcome in the land of the *Nnee.*

Though the event with the Apache had been worrisome,

it turned out to provide them with a new level of confidence. Pang rode with his head higher, looking about the wilderness with interest, curiosity, and an alert eye. The Apache riders who now accompanied them also provided strength in numbers. Though Geronimo had told them about the posse that looked for Valdar, Enrique was certain that the Apache way of tracking and capture was more dependable than any civic procedure of the Anglo settlements.

The Apache were on mounts from their own remuda—which Enrique believed were likely confiscated or stolen—but that was the Apache way. One of the braves, Perro Alto (Tall Dog), rode a bay mare and carried his repeating rifle in a deerskin scabbard. He was an excellent tracker, which was why Geronimo had sent him. He was named for his slender frame, taller than most Apache, and for his ability to sniff out the enemy.

The other brave, Torro Rapido (Quick Bull), rode a black-and-white paint, mostly white, and always held his rifle. Geronimo had said he was quick to shoot, which was not always good, but might be in their pursuit of the Demon Warrior.

They rode for two days and crossed the Pedregosa, and Tall Dog led them to two mounds of dirt. He dismounted, grabbed a handful of soil from a mound, and sniffed it.

"Fresh graves," he said. "Two days."

The Apache walked around, inspecting the ground, then pointed northwest. "Many riders, head that way." Then he pointed east. "Other riders, look like eight, go that way." Then he pointed northeast. "But lone rider go that way."

Enrique was positive the posse had had a confrontation with Valdar, which explained part of the division. But the solitary rider he couldn't understand. "One rider?" Enrique said. "Why just one?"

"Whoever he is, he hides in the Pedregosa," Tall Dog said.

Dutton squatted and placed on a roasting skewer some back-strap slices, which were of a deer he'd killed the prior evening. He'd spotted the doe along with two yearlings foraging near a mountain draw. They were at least two hundred yards away, but he knew he had just as much chance with a long shot as he did trying to get closer and challenge their keen senses. Unfortunately he gut-shot the doe and had to track her blood trail another hundred yards before finding her dead farther down the draw. He hated the thought of an animal suffering and always did his best to make a quick kill. On the trail he couldn't prepare all the meat; he could only take what he could eat that night. The coyotes, buzzards and crows would certainly find their prize on his behalf.

He moved the coals in the fire around until the flames shot higher onto the meat. He rose quickly as his horse, tied behind him, let out an alerting whicker.

As he looked at the horse, he noticed it peering off to the south, its ears turned forward like thistle cones, capturing whatever had alerted its senses. That's when Dutton spotted the Apache, sitting on a bay horse on a distant bluff, the morning light highlighting specific details of the brave's features: his hair, his skin, his breechcloth, his rifle.

Dutton stood there in a staring contest, and out of the corner of his eye he noticed his horse's head move. Another Apache, on a black-and-white paint, appeared farther east, on another bluff, with his rifle aimed at the sheriff.

Dutton fell to the ground quickly then crawled behind a boulder. He pulled his six-gun and peered back over the boulder. Both Apaches were gone.

"What the—"

Moments later he saw four riders coming into camp, two on mules with a pack burro trailing, and the two Apaches trailing behind. He stood slowly, his six-gun still in his hand but held down.

"Who goes there?" he said.

"We come in peace," said the lead rider, who appeared to be a Mexican wearing a sombrero and serape.

As they rode into camp, the lead rider dismounted, and as Dutton gave a hard look at the second rider, he recognized the face. "You're that Chinaman—Pang Lo."

"I am," Pang said. "You cannot arrest me now."

"I don't plan to," Dutton said, holstering his revolver.

All but the Apaches gathered at the fire. The sheriff invited them to share his meal, and Enrique tried to convince the Apaches to join them. The three of them talked over coffee (donated by the new riders) and fire-roasted venison, and then shared their knowledge and experiences and agreed to work together to find and kill Valdar. Tall Dog and Quick Bull eventually dismounted, after Enrique coaxed them with the sight of the steaming backstrap.

"I can't figure how someone can be so wicked," Dutton said.

The Apaches continued to eat vigorously, taking large bites of the meat and licking their fingers. Pang did not eat much of the meat, just warmed his hands over the fire. Enrique had finished eating and was washing the meal down with fresh coffee, for which Dutton expressed his gratitude.

"Father Gaeta said he is the work of Satan," Enrique said. "No good can come from him."

"I'm not so sure Satan could beat this feller," Dutton said. "He's one bad *hombre*."

"Where do you think he is now?" Enrique said.

"I'd say he's at least two days ahead of us," Dutton said, "but he'll ride much slower with those women."

Pang looked up at them. "Then we should ride faster."

"We will, son," Dutton said. "As fast as our mounts will let us."

"Don't worry," Enrique said. "We are much stronger now, being six instead of five."

Dutton squinted, calculating in his head. "Six?"

Enrique grinned. "Ah, but you have not met Sereno, our desert watchman who is out there but does not ride with us."

Dutton gazed out across the mountain slopes. "All right, I'll have to take your word for that one."

Dutton looked out at the horizon, the pinkish haze fading away to a brilliant blue. He couldn't help but smile, thinking of how he had hoped for an answer, and it amused him to think that it had come to him in four languages: English, Spanish, Apache, and Chinese.

Valdar and his *compadres* ran into a camp of three renegade Apache, and they shared their tequila and opium. It was not hard to convince them to join up with Valdar, especially after they raided a small settlement of Mexicans, killed the men, raped the women, ate their food, and took their horses and a young girl at the age of puberty. They kept her pure, however, knowing that a young virgin would bring a premium price.

Their night camp was always a fiesta, with tequila and opium, but Valdar made it very clear the women were off limits. "They must be clean when we cross the border," he said. "If they are not, I lose money, and I do not like to lose money."

One of the renegade Apache slipped off into the darkness to relieve himself, and he came back with a prisoner. The sight of this young Indian made Valdar lose his rheumy smile and rise to his feet.

"Where did you find him?" Valdar said, noticing blood on the boy's pant leg.

"He was watching me piss," the Apache said. "He tried to run away, but I threw my knife into his leg. He could not run anymore."

Valdar walked up to the boy, grabbed him by his chin, and lifted his face up to look in his eyes. "He looks harmless." Then Valdar suddenly smiled. "Ah, there is a man in Chihuahua that likes boys, and he pays well." As he looked the young Indian over, he pushed the boy's head sideways and noticed the scar on his neck. "Hmm, someone tried to finish this one off and they failed. Are you a troublemaker, *Papagito*?" Valdar lost his smile. "It could be that you are a lucky one. Well, I assure you, your luck has run out."

Enrique rode next to Dutton the entire day, leading the new posse into the New Mexico Territory. He liked this Sheriff Dutton, and he wasn't sure if it was because of his steadfast, willing nature or the respect he seemed to show them all.

Regardless, it was nice to have the extra man, whose duty fit the same purpose.

Pang was also glad to have the sheriff along, and believed the man's desire to help him was now genuine. He understood how difficult it would have been, if not impossible, to show his support back in Tucson. But it was as if the dream of vengeance he had had was now coming true, only in a different fashion than he had wanted. He supposed it did not matter, so long as the end result, the recovery of his sister and fiancée, along with the destruction of Valdar, took place.

After riding for nearly two hours, mostly in silence, just absorbing the new energy and terrain, Dutton wondered what drove these men. Pang he understood, but he knew nothing about Enrique Osorio, or the two Apache. When he asked, Enrique told him how the Demon Warrior had betrayed Geronimo's tribe.

"You know Geronimo?" the sheriff asked.

"Recently acquainted." He held up his hand and showed him the scar on his palm. "We are now blood brothers."

Dutton told him about the run-in he had recently had with Geronimo, and Enrique told him that Geronimo seemed to be a reasonable man.

"So long as you are with us, and pursuing Valdar, Geronimo will not bother you."

"That's easy for you to say," Dutton said. "You're not affiliated with the white man's government. He hates it like no other."

Dutton finally asked why Enrique was on this pursuit, and after a deep breath, Enrique gave him the short version of what had happened to his family, but the short version did not leave out the words "rape" and "cold-blooded murder."

"Father Gaeta tried very hard to keep me from this journey," Enrique said, "but he finally gave in, and told me that only God's will can prevail."

"Well, if it's any comfort, if I'd have been through what you have, a desert storm couldn't have stopped me from going."

Enrique looked at the sheriff gravely. "The desert storm is about to come."

Dutton thought long and hard about these two young men and what they'd gone through, and a chill ran up his spine. It was even a greater chill when he learned about how the two men came together. Fate, he thought, was an incredible thing, and the most vivid evidence of it, like Pang and Enrique together, should have been enough to convince any man that these things do not happen by mere chance.

They rode on, and eventually Enrique wanted to know more about the sheriff. "Father Gaeta was the only white man I ever knew. What brought you here, Sheriff?"

"Darn restless feet I reckon," the sheriff said, looking down at the rocky terrain. "My parents settled in Missouri and farmed eighty acres. I fought for the Union Army in the War Between the States, was only eighteen, barely escaped death a few times, and have the scars to prove it. I suppose it was that war that changed me. For some reason I couldn't go back to Missouri and be a farmer. I tried, but the simple life had left my blood. I wanted to try something different. I went to Saint Joseph, almost went west from there, but a poster advertising the Santa Fe Trail lured me to Westport. A scout on the trail kept talking about the thousands of acres of land in the new territories, raw and lawless, just waiting to be settled and tamed for cattle ranching, and that image never left my mind. It was just what my restless mind yearned for."

"Did you stay in touch with your *mamá* and *papá*?"

"We exchanged a few letters. My pa died two years ago. Ma said they buried him down the road, in a community cemetery. She said that my brother was running the farm now and had bought another a hundred and sixty acres. My heart hurt a little, but I have never regretted leaving. I get a letter occasionally from my brother. He tells me how well he's doing, and that it sure would be good if I'd come back. Half of the old farm is still mine, he said. And that if I'd come, we'd buy more."

"Do you want to go back?" Enrique said.

"Don't know how I could. With all I have to do here, I can't think about nothing else."

"I've never thought about anything but killing Valdar. I cannot imagine justice without seeing his own blood on my hands. One time the priest asked me when that was over, what I would do. That was the first time I had ever thought of such a thing. I've never imagined my life without my search for justice."

"Well, I'm sure it will come to you," the sheriff said. "One thing at a time. If we make it through this alive, then we'll all decide what's next for us."

Dutton was quite taken by his newfound confidence. He knew that it was partly because of the spirit and will that consumed all these men, a combined energy that was more powerful than he could have ever generated with the posse that retreated. Enrique and Pang, he knew, would never give in, and would carry on until the end. Something he knew he would have to do, too, and now he wouldn't have to do it alone.

By the end of the day Enrique was worried about Sereno, or about what Sereno might have discovered. He usually spotted him a half a dozen times or more during a day, but today he hadn't seen him but twice. These occurrences took place in the early part of the day, and it was now near dusk and the Tohono O'odham had made no presence known. Enrique let the rest of the crew know of his concern, and to be aware that maybe Sereno had found something and was in hiding. This had them all prepared to do some nighttime prowling for the Valdar camp.

"They could be tying one on," Dutton said, "so we can listen carefully for the sounds of laughing. But be careful, being drunk don't mean they won't be dangerous."

"They were drunk when they killed my family," Enrique said.

"Yes," Pang said. "Their tequila and opium are what gives them their evil strength. I would rather attack them in the morning, when their heads are hurting and their eyes are blurry and bloodshot."

"That's not a bad idea there, Pang," Dutton said. "You boys just lead the way, and I'll back you up."

The finding of the Indian boy in the desert spooked Valdar. His drunken frenzy ended as he had Baliador take the boy and put him with the other prisoners, and he told his *compadre* that he was now in charge. It was a common move that his sidekicks were used to. He either left the gang for some kind of desert spiritual gathering, the communication with his demon spirits, or to go on ahead for other arrangements, specifically business. Being so close to El Paso, they knew the latter was likely his move. He took all the horses they had taken from the posse members and the Mexicans, tied them together in a line, and off he went into the darkness.

Times like these were special moments for Baliador. His first move was to make sure all captive merchandise was accounted for and well constrained, and then to make sure Beshkah was passed out drunk. With him out, he could do anything he wanted.

It took two hours to smoke enough opium and pour enough tequila down the renegade to get him where Baliador wanted him. They were standing together, relieving themselves, when Beshkah fell over forward and vomited. He lay there moaning, and seconds later he was snoring.

Baliador dropped the half-empty bottle of tequila next to his *compadre* and went to the other Apache who had joined them. They, too, were out like sleeping babies, snoring next to the campfire. Baliador kicked one of them lightly, and he only grunted and went back to snoring. The renegade grinned and walked on to his purpose.

They were tied together, waist to waist, behind a cluster of boulders near the camp, with the lead rope tied to a piñon. Their wrists and ankles were also tied together, but the ankles only when they camped.

The Tohono O'odham boy was now at the end of their chain and was the first to see the renegade as he walked up on them. The boy scooted back as Baliador approached, but Baliador paid him no mind. The next was the Mexican girl, who slept with her head on the lap of Mun Lo, who slept with her head on the shoulder of Sai Min. Sai Min slept in a sitting position, her head tilted back on the boulder, but she awakened and gasped when she saw Baliador squatting in front of her, staring, smiling.

He grabbed her by the front of her robe, now soiled and torn in many places from the rough trek across the desert and into the mountains. She screamed and cried, and the other women woke and did the same. The renegade did not even untie Sai Min, as that posed an unnecessary risk; he pulled her to her back, crawled on top of her, and opened her robe.

She let out a frightful scream, lifted up swiftly her tied-together wrists and fists, and struck Baliador under the chin. His head went back sharply, but came back to look at her with an angry stare as quick as it had gone back. He slapped her across the face and she cried, as did Mun Lo, who hit him on the back. Baliador would take nothing from her either and swung his hand sideways, knocking her down. She looked up at him with tearful eyes, and blood trickled from her lip onto her chin, which, like her face, was soiled, the white makeup mostly faded away.

The renegade looked back down at Sai Min, at her undergarments, and how difficult they would be to remove without tearing. He wanted her badly, as he'd never been with a Chinese woman, but to tear her garments was sure to give Valdar a clue to her having been touched. Baliador was not afraid of Valdar, but he liked his position and how much he learned of the known Demon Warrior's business practices. One day he would go off on his own, but he still had much to learn and did not want to jeopardize it now.

In frustration he pulled Sai Min's robe closed, jumped back up, and knowing the other China girl would be the same, he went to the Mexican. He pulled her to her back and lifted her dress, and just as he had thought—no undergarments. But then he realized that the buyer in Mexico would know if she was not a virgin. How this man could tell, Baliador did not know, but Valdar knew her as a virgin and would expect her to be that way when selling time came. Even more frustrated, Baliador jumped away and yelled. The women huddled together and cried, and Sereno backed closer to the wall, his arms tight against his chest, his hands in fists over his mouth, and his big eyes staring at the renegade.

Baliador could not understand how men could be with other men. He had heard Valdar comment that he found pleasure in it but preferred women more. There were occasions when Valdar would find a virgin girl and have her for himself. A bonus he would allow himself to have, but not very often. In fact, it had only happened three times since the time Baliador had joined up with him. The last time was a white girl, maybe twelve years old, whom they'd captured from a family whose wagon was traveling across the desert, likely on its way to California. Valdar took her, Baliador supposed, because she was a blonde, which, untouched or not, brought a premium.

The time before that was another Mexican girl, who Valdar said reminded him of his mother. And the time before that was with a Tohono O'odham girl, who fought so much that the only way Valdar could get her tamed down was to rape her. Plus, Valdar had said, he liked it when they fought, it gave him the deepest pleasure.

The renegade decided that his luck would not prevail this

time, and that it was not worth any risk to have any of the women. He certainly couldn't do anything with the boy, so he would wait until El Paso, or until they raided another camp. With such a feeling of defeat, there was only one thing to do, so he went back to the campfire, found a bottle of tequila and an opium pipe, and sat down next to the snoring Apache and returned to the world of euphoria.

The dawn of the desert was typically a peaceful time, where one could say good-bye to the nocturnal voices and take pleasure in the birds and their morning songs and the hazy pastels of the sky with their brilliance cast on the mountain-side. But the men, with their minds on their pursuit, were looking at nothing but the aftereffects of evil and trying not to let their anger take away from their abilities. Father Gaeta had warned that it could happen, and when Enrique had passed on this wisdom to the others, Pang agreed, and said that his father would have said the same thing.

After Tall Dog had scouted the camp, he reported back to them with alarming news.

"Your watchman is tied up with the women, but they are all there."

Pang and Enrique made solemn eye contact. "This is our moment," Enrique said.

Pang nodded.

"The Demon Warrior is not there," Tall Dog said.

They all looked back at him.

"What are you saying?" Enrique said.

"He is not in the camp. There are only the traitors of the *Nnee*. All are sleeping."

"Why is Valdar not there?" Enrique said through his teeth.

"He must be moving on ahead of the gang," Dutton said. "We are getting closer to El Paso."

"This is better for us," Pang said. "We can capture our women; that way they are safe. Then we will go on and find Valdar. It will be only him, because all of his men will be dead."

"Pang's got a good point there," Dutton said. "He's one less man we'd have to fight now, and he'll be much easier to handle alone."

"All right," Enrique said. "It is us against two. Our odds are better."

"You are mistaken," Tall Dog said. "There are four Apache."

"Four?"

"I recognized two others who did not pass their bravery tests and Geronimo would not let them serve as warriors to the *Nnee*. They left the tribe and swore vengeance on our chief."

"Ah, I see," Enrique said. "They are wanting help from the Demon Warrior to seek their vengeance. Well, we will not give them a chance."

All nodded in agreement with Enrique, and the men sat together and formed their plan. After the plan was made, each man prepared himself.

The sheriff made sure his gun belt was full of cartridges, and the gun itself was loaded. He spun the cylinder, then looked out over the sight. His gun was ready.

Pang walked aside from the group, and began squatting up and down slowly, leaning from side to side, one leg long, the other bent underneath him. Then he stretched his arms, above his head and down to his toes. During all, he breathed deeply, in and out. Then he practiced kicking, from the front and the side, and jabbing with his hands, up, down, and from side to side. When he knelt to the ground and put his hands in a praying position, he, too, was ready.

Enrique checked that he had enough arrows—the longer, straightest arrows, with ends sharp and deadly. He made sure his quiver was full, and that the string on his bow was sure and tight. When all was checked, Enrique, like the others, was ready.

Tall Dog and Quick Bull sat holding their rifles and watching the others, occasionally pointing and sharing some observation they had made about the styles of fighting the men chose. They took particular interest in Pang, and Enrique understood that they were quite taken by his art. He also knew that they had nothing to do to prepare, that the Apache were used to fighting and always ready.

The men surrounded the camp, which was near the bank of a desert wash between the mountains. There wasn't a lot to hide behind in such an arid place, but the desert floor was like a maze of plants, shrubs, and cacti, and with enough cunning and careful planning, sneaking up on enemies was not impossible.

Tall Dog and Quick Bull took higher positions at the base of the mountains, fifty yards from camp. Their main purpose was to have their rifles ready to shoot down the men as they woke, and to protect the women and Sereno.

Enrique took a similar position, only closer, behind a stand of mesquite, from where he could see the faces of the men, and Sheriff Dutton, of course, as he worked his way into the camp. Enrique would also protect Pang, who, after he released the women, would wake the renegades from their sleep and release a style of fury unlike anything they'd ever seen. After Tall Dog explained to them the fighting abilities, or lack thereof, of the two new Apache members, they all agreed that Baliador and Beshkah were the biggest threat, and that Beshkah was likely the most dangerous of the remaining two.

Pang stepped quietly around the rocks and peeked at the prisoners. Sereno saw him instantly and the Chinaman held a finger over his mouth. The Tohono O'odham nudged the girl next to him, and she alerted Sai and Mun, and they all looked on in wonder and cried when they saw Pang. As he had with Sereno, he quickly signaled to them to remain still and silent.

He looked back around to make sure the sheriff was near his position, and then the Chinaman stepped nimbly toward the prisoners. He pulled a knife from a sheath given to him by Tall Dog and cut them free. Sereno wasted no time and ran off, while Mun and Sai embraced Pang and cried. The Mexican girl rubbed her wrists. She stared at Pang and expressed her gratitude with a weeping voice. Pang did not understand her Spanish tongue, but she understood his motions when he encouraged them to run away.

"You are coming with us?" Sai Min said.

"I will join you shortly. You run, I will find you."

They tried to argue with him, but he would not hear it. They hugged him tight, then ran away weeping.

Dutton looked over at Beshkah, who lay moaning several feet from the smoking campfire, and at the others in their drunken slumber. He took notice of the spurs on Beshkah's boots, and the shiny plates on the toes. Never had he seen such strange weapons, which were enough to know just how crazy the man was.

He looked up to verify the positions of the other men, and spotted Tall Dog and Quick Bull, and then Enrique, who looked with one eye down an arrow. Dutton grabbed a handful of sand and stood above Beshkah's face. The renegade's mouth was slightly agape as he snored. The sheriff sifted the sand between the fingers of his fist and onto Beshkah's open lips. Beshkah's eyes twitched and his mouth closed. He raised his head slowly, his eyes still closed, and began spitting the sand from his mouth. He rose to his elbows, his eyes opened to a slight squint, and when he saw Dutton, he jumped to his feet.

Enrique's arrow made a thud in the renegade's breastbone. He looked at it, then grabbed it with both hands, growled, clenched his teeth, and pulled it out. Blood immediately followed, as did another arrow that stuck in his neck. This time the Apache fell to his knees, his eyes glaring at Dutton and his hands on the arrow in his neck. But he did not have the strength to remove this one, and fell dead in front of them.

Pang made his presence known with the sheriff at the camp. He took one step back, crouched into his fighting stance, with legs slightly bent and hands out in front of his chest. Baliador awoke and rose to his feet. The Chinaman offered him a slight smirk. Without any more hesitation, Baliador growled and kicked a leg forward, but Pang was quick to divert it, and the Apache fell forward clumsily. Annoyed, he got back up and wasted no time lunging for the Chinaman again, only this time with his arms wide and a distorting grimace.

Dutton held his gun with a steady aim and was about to pull the trigger when he heard a gunshot and looked to the base of the mountains where their Apache friends were posted. To his dismay he saw that Tall Dog lay facedown over the edge of some protruding rocks, his arms dangling and blood running from underneath him. Quick Bull rose to shoot but was quickly gunned down as well. All watched in confusion; the other renegades awoke, and then suddenly, out of the desert maze the culprit made his presence known, with Mun Lo in his grasp.

He yelled into the camp in a heckling tone. "Ah, does this mess up your plans, *amigos*?"

Valdar shot again, toward Enrique, and the shot ricocheted off the rock. "How about laying down your bow, *Papagito*, and stepping out from behind there. Of course, I could just cut this woman's throat and then we could fight it out and see who wins." He turned to the sheriff. "You, too, *oficial*. Drop that weapon. And convince your chink friend there to keep his hands and feet to himself."

Enrique stood slowly and laid down his bow. Pang stood grimacing and breathing hard, and Dutton dropped his gun. Baliador and the other two Apache quickly subdued them all, grabbing them by the backs of their necks and kicking the backs of their knees to buckle them to the ground. Baliador supplied enough rope to tie them all together, back to back, by the wrists.

"What an interesting bunch you are," Valdar said, standing in front of them with a sobbing Mun Lo in his clutches.

"A Chinaman who has a lot of guts, I must say, to come all this way for his women."

He looked at the sheriff. "You must be the lawman who lost his posse." Valdar laughed wildly and shoved Mun Lo to Baliador, then knelt down in front of Enrique. He looked at him through eyes that were bloodshot and yellow.

"But who is this *Papagito*?" They looked hard at each other. "Aye, something is familiar about you, but I do not know. Like so many, I suppose you, too, have some kind of beef with the Demon Warrior, no?"

"*Sic semper cum judicium et cruor*," Enrique said. He wasn't sure whether Valdar knew Latin, but the expression seemed fitting. *Thus always with judgment and blood.*

Valdar lost his smug grin and walked away. Baliador pulled Mun Lo along, and the Apaches followed. Pang squirmed nervously in their confinement.

"What the hell do we do now?" Dutton said.

"We are lucky we are still alive," Enrique said.

"But for what reason?" Dutton said. "If Valdar gets the best of you, he doesn't let you live unless he needs you for something."

"I was thinking the same thing," Enrique said. "But I can't explain it."

"I know," Pang said as he watched Valdar and his men subdue Mun Lo once again. "Sai Min is still free. He will use us to get her back."

"*Sí*, that makes sense," Enrique said. "We have to figure out a way to spoil those plans."

"She will come back for us," Pang said. "If we are alive, she will stay close. If we are dead, she will run."

"I wish we could get word to her to stay away," Dutton said.

"Sereno went free, yes?" Enrique said.

"Yes," Pang said.

"He will not stray far. He is our hope."

"I hope you're right," Dutton said. "Right now we need a miracle."

"To be alive at this point is a miracle in itself," Enrique said.

It was almost dark again when the three men had received only the beginning of what could be the horrifying wrath of the Demon Warrior. Valdar and the Apache celebrated with tequila, wine, and opium. They laughed and cursed God, and made frequent visits to the three men. They spat and urinated on them. They kicked off their hats and stomped them to shreds. One time Baliador threatened Pang with a knife, bringing it to his face and running it underneath his nose. There was a slight sting and a little blood, which ran down the crevices of his lips and into his mouth, but the knife left only a scratch. If Baliador had wanted to hurt him, he could have done so with ease. It, like the acts of the others, was nothing but torment.

All the while, they struggled with their tied hands. Pang kept trying to work his hands loose, but many times when the visits came, they would check the knots and secure them.

There was one occasion when Valdar came and paid Pang and Dutton no mind, but sat down next to Enrique with tequila in hand. In all his drunkenness he put his arm around Enrique. The foulness of Valdar's dirty, sweaty armpit made the muscles in Enrique's throat tighten and bile rise. Valdar's breath was no better, but Enrique figured that he'd gotten used to the stench of their urine and it had helped him tolerate the rest.

"Why is it, *Papagito*, that I cannot place you?" Valdar said in a slur.

Enrique did not answer, but he was able to offer a slight grin.

Valdar laughed. "Ahhh, you are trying to make me guess. But I have thought long about it, and I do not know. Where do you come from?"

"Maybe I am the great Lucifer himself," Enrique said. "I have come to check up on my children."

Valdar laughed again. "Very good, *Papagito*. No, no, if you were him, I would not have been able to tie you up."

"Maybe you have not yet met my wrath. Maybe this is a great foreplay to your stinking blood being swallowed by the earth."

Valdar grabbed Enrique's chin, squeezed it hard, and stared squarely into his eyes. "Who the hell are you!"

Enrique said nothing, and Valdar slapped him with the back of his hand, and then stood and kicked him in the stomach. The smart on his face made no measure to the blunt, dull pain in his abdomen. He clenched his teeth and tried to wish the pain away.

"To hell with you," Valdar said. "You may not tell me now, but I will find out. And when I do, your death will be one more painful than any I've ever given. *Sí*, you can count on it."

Valdar kicked Enrique again in the thigh and then walked away.

When it was finally dark, the three men watched on,

weary and cold, as the renegades continued their nightly ritual of euphoria and entertained Valdar with jokes about one another, often about their mothers. None ever took offense, until Baliador called one of the new Apaches a brainless yellow dog, and the Apache tried to avenge himself. But Baliador simply pushed him away and he landed in the fire. They all laughed heartily as he got up and rolled on the ground to put out the fire in his hair and clothes.

"We've got to get out of this," Dutton said, squirming for comfort.

"I've been trying," Pang said, "but your hands are below mine, and the knots are too tight. They've tied us brilliantly."

"I just hope they don't kill us 'brilliantly,'" Dutton said.

A noise came from the darkness, and one that Enrique did not recognize.

"What was that?" Dutton said.

"I don't know," Enrique said. "It isn't one of Sereno's calls."

"I know what it was," Pang said. "It is Sai Min. She has come back for us."

"How on earth is a China girl going to help us?" Dutton said.

"Do not underestimate the strength of our women, Sheriff. They study and learn many of the same arts as we men do."

"All right, then. But I'll believe it when I see us clear of this hell."

They heard nothing more from Sai, until a rock flew in to them and hit Pang in the shoulder.

"What the—" Dutton said.

"It is her!" Pang said.

"No," Enrique said with a smile. "It is our watchman."

"Well . . . where the hell is he?" Dutton said.

They next thing they heard was commotion in the camp, and they noticed that all the men stood and looked off into the darkness. Then Sai Min appeared, walking toward them in slow strides, dressed only in her undergarments, and the top unbuttoned midway down her chest.

"Oh, Sai, no!" Pang said.

"She is sacrificing herself for us," Enrique said.

Pang squirmed, turned his wrists, and shouted angrily. "No, she is not!"

One thing that the men noticed was that the renegades gave her their attention quickly, but Valdar only stood and stared, and then looked at them. That is when they knew that Valdar would not fall for Sai Min's ploy. An improperly dressed woman might be a weakness to some men, but Valdar was the master of overcoming such weaknesses. His demons would not allow him to let lustful desires interfere with his reason.

Before any of the renegades laid a hand on her, Sai Min's thin, pale body took a stance that was only familiar to Pang, and in her quickness she jabbed and kicked, sending all three drunken Apaches to the ground. They staggered up in a state of stupor, but Sai was quick to send them back to the ground and, before long, unconsciousness.

Valdar would stand for no more. He pulled his revolver, but it was quickly taken from his hand by a stone. He looked around in frustration and another hit him in the forehead. He lay on the ground moaning.

"Now what do we do?" Dutton said.

Sai Min started toward them, and that was when Mun

Lo made her presence known, dashing quickly toward the men as well. Both of the women slid to their knees on the desert ground near Pang.

Pang looked up at them both with great joy. "Mun Lo, how did you get loose?"

She smiled, but suddenly covered her mouth and nose from the stench of the urine. "Sai Min untied me. Now, if I can stand it, I will untie you."

She did so, and when they were free, Pang quickly embraced Sai Min, but suddenly Valdar appeared in front of them. His eyes revealed a frightful anger as he lunged for Pang's fiancée and tackled her to the ground. He rose again with a knife to her throat.

"I have had enough of you people! Stop or I will kill her."

The three men stood slowly in wonder as Valdar crawfished backward with Sai Min in his clutches.

"You go!" Sai Min cried, under the pressure of the point of Valdar's knife at her neck.

"We cannot leave you!" Pang said.

"Spare your own lives! Go!"

"She is right," Enrique said. "Besides, I think Valdar is bluffing. She is too valuable. He won't kill her."

"I cannot take that chance," Pang said.

"Think about it!" Enrique said. "I know it sounds cruel. But she has saved us all with her bravery. We should honor her work."

"Enrique's right," Dutton said, putting his hand on Pang's shoulder. "Let's make a new plan and come back for her."

Pang stood in dismay and looked on as the Demon Warrior restrained his beloved. "We will be back for you!"

"You will be back for a dead woman!" Valdar said. "And you will die yourselves!"

They all turned and ran into the darkness. They ran as far as they could in the night, using Enrique's expert guidance. They eventually slowed as they stepped into a higher altitude. They held on to one another by gripping their belts, and Mun Lo took the rear holding on to her brother. After more than two hours they stopped, short of breath from the lower oxygen. Enrique told them to sit tight as he gathered wood for a fire.

"What if Valdar sees our fire?" Pang said.

"It won't matter," Dutton said. "He knows we're out here, but he won't try anything until the renegades are up and healthy. He is less of a threat without Beshkah. It may not seem so, my friends, but we won the battle. It's the war that is not yet won."

Pang embraced his sister, and she clung to him, forgiving his stench, her head resting on his shoulder.

"I would die for you," he said.

She held him tighter and closed her eyes. "I thought I would never see you again."

"You will never have that worry . . . ever again."

When Enrique returned and built a fire, and they sat in silence for most of the night. They were too afraid, and too anxious, to sleep, but also too weary to move on.

Pang pushed at the glowing embers with the sole of his boot and stoked the fire. He looked at Enrique. "You know, it's amazing how our dreams change."

They all looked at him.

"I remember when I was a child coming to America. I

was only six. My father had worked out an arrangement with the railroad. They paid for our passage to California if we would work for them. I remember being hungry back in China. I would help my mother pick up the rice grains in the fields that other people had dropped, just so we could have something to eat. But there were days we did not eat at all. America would change all that. But we sacrificed our family to have it. We made a good living in Tucson, and kept trying to send for my mother, but the American laws kept us from bringing her. Mun Lo and Sai Min were smuggled here, and my father paid well to have it done. We were so close to our dream. Now my father is dead. My mother will probably never see us again. And I fight for the life of my Sai Min. What once was a dream of life is now a dream of blood."

They all looked at the fire soberly, and Mun once again hugged her brother.

"You are right, *mi amigo*," Enrique said. "I was too young to know how good things really were. Too young, really, to have known I was taking it all for granted. But since my family was killed, and my sister taken away, I have had only one dream, and it is that same dream for blood."

Pang nodded, as did Dutton.

"I think we should try our attack before dawn," Dutton said.

They all looked at him blankly.

"Valdar won't be expecting that," Dutton said. "And the renegades will still be sore and hungover. And if you think about it, how will we get out of here without horses or mules? He has our mounts, our supplies, and our weapons. We have to get them back."

Enrique looked at Pang for approval. The Chinaman nodded.

"But how will we attack without weapons?" Enrique said.

Pang stood. "It is not the weapon that fights, but the mind and the body. I know how we can do it."

"Okay," Enrique said. "We have less than four hours until dawn. We should go now, to the base of the mountain, where the air is better. We can have an hour's rest before we attack."

The group made their plan, then nothing more was said. Enrique went off to pray, Pang and Mun Lo to meditate, and when they came back they all descended the mountain together, nearly as weary as when they had come up, and anticipating another gray dawn.


The hour that they rested seemed like an eternity, and though their bodies were not active, their minds felt no more relaxed. They sat less than one hundred yards from Valdar's camp, with no fire to keep them warm, but still and quiet among the rocks and junipers.

Enrique thought long and hard about how, thus far, the events had turned out. It was Beshkah and Baliador who killed his parents. It satisfied him some to know that Beshkah was now dead, and by his own arrows. His mission, in part, was a third in completion. But revenge still burned inside him, and he knew, too, that the most difficult part was yet to come.

Enrique did not worry about Sereno anymore. If anyone knew desert survival, it was Sereno. He did hope, however, that the Tohono O'odham would go back to the mission. If they captured him once, they could do it again, and like Father Gaeta, Sereno was nearly all the family he had left.

Since both Pang and his sister had the talent of kung fu, they all agreed that the brother and sister would do the combating while Enrique and the sheriff gathered the mules and horses, and other things if they could find them. The horses, they agreed, were the most important, and with them they could ride to a village to replace their weapons and supplies. But without them, survival in such a remote and barren land would be much more difficult.

When dawn approached and Pang and Mun Lo snuck into the camp, it was empty, with only the dwindling remains of a campfire and flies swarming over the dead, blood-soaked body of Beshkah. Enrique and Dutton watched for their signal, only to have the two return with the bad news. They all walked around the camp, and Enrique found where many horse and mule prints indicated they had ridden southeast out of the camp. Enrique found the charred remains of his bow and quiver of arrows in the fire. Dutton picked up the burned edge of his hat brim. They looked at one another, realizing by their grave faces that they were stranded without horses, without weapons for hunting food, and without the proper desert attire.

"What the hell do we do now?" Dutton said.

"We walk," Enrique said.

"Where to?"

"Until we find horses."

"And you know where some are?"

"No, but we must have faith."

"Faith?"

"Yes, Sheriff, faith. After all this, you are still alive, aren't you?"

Judging by his defeated look, the sheriff would not challenge Enrique on this point. "All right, so what's your plan?"

"We go southeast. Regardless of our difference in pace, we will still gain ground. All the while we look for trails. When we find a trail, we will find a settlement with horses and supplies."

No one argued with Enrique's plan, and as he walked southeast out of the camp, they all followed. After they'd been walking for two hours, the sun began to beat down harder on them. Enrique figured that it was a necessary time for water and searched for a barrel cactus and yucca. He showed them the technique he had learned, but warned them that if they got too hot, only to wet their mouths and swallow very little, and they followed his instruction.

By mid-afternoon they had stopped only once more, again for water, and even Enrique had never experienced such a vulnerable time in the desert. Mun Lo collapsed once, and they shaded her and gave her time to recover before they moved on. While they rested, Enrique took the time to find tall grasses and reeds to make a snare, and eventually he caught a rabbit and three quail. He brought them back and dressed them, and later that evening they made camp and made a meal of his kill. They slept in the coolness of the night air and rose early to continue on.

The new day brought more heat, thirst, and fatigue than the day before, and after half a day of walking, with only one stop for water, it took both the sheriff and Pang to hold up Mun Lo and keep her going. Each step was a struggle, where their feet felt heavier and harder to lift and move forward. The heat fell heavy on their hatless heads and scorched their faces to a dry and cracking redness. Before long, the sheriff lost his balance and all three fell. Enrique turned to them, and with exhaustion and sorrow for their misery, he fell to his knees.

The Sonora and all the regions around it were tough lands to reckon with, and few knew it all as well as Enrique. Only his Apache neighbors, who were as much a part of the land as the trees, plants, and rocks, knew better how to survive the desert. Enrique found it amusing when a gringo who passed through figured all he needed was a good supply of water. Hydration was important, but the sun and protection from it was what one needed to consider most. A hat shaded the face from too much heat, as did loose clothing of light color, and a tree was a desert traveler's best friend. It just so happened that they had fallen into an area of the lowlands far from any trees or streams and their hats were taken by Valdar and thrown into his fire. The protection they needed was nowhere near.

Enrique thought about removing a serape, or shirt, or some garment to lay over Mun Lo and protect her face from the sun, but it was too dangerous to expose any skin. Their faces were already red and would likely blister. Enrique looked up into the bright sky, and reminiscent of the day when he was a boy and tried to bury his parents' bodies, the long beams of sunlight came down upon him. He knew he was too far away for the priest to save him now.

He looked back at his friends, who lay exhausted and weak. He rose slowly to his feet, searched, and found more barrel cactus and gave water to each of his friends in a curled agave leaf. He dropped water into Mun Lo's mouth and rubbed it on her cracked lips. She winced at the pain. He gave water to the others, too. Not much, but just enough to soothe their dry mouths and throats.

Enrique looked at the sheriff, who sat with his knees against his chest, his arms around his knees, and his face buried between them. Then he looked at Pang, who held his sister's head in his lap and wept. It was the first time since they had met that Pang appeared defeated. A feeling that Enrique knew he had to avoid for himself.

# DON RICHARD BENJAMIN

When he woke, it was to the sound of whickering. His eyes peeked open to a blurry image of men in wide sombreros lifting his friends onto horses. He thought it was a mirage until he felt his own body being lifted and draped over another man's shoulder, then propped up on one of the animals. Enrique fell forward and rested his head on the horse's mane. The horn of the saddle pushed sharply into his chest. He hardly had the strength to open his eyes, let alone raise his head, so he lay there, with the smell of the horse and saddle leather in his nose—the smell of salvation.

The next time he woke, he was being carried into a cool adobe and laid in a bed. He could hear voices in both Spanish and English, but still did not have the strength to rise up and acknowledge who was speaking. He felt his clothes being removed, and a cool cloth dabbed over his forehead. He opened his eyes slightly to see the face of a frail old Mexican woman. She moved the cloth away, and he heard her wringing out water, then felt it drop onto his dry, parted lips.

At first the water stung, but eventually it felt good, as it did when she wiped it over his body. He wasn't sure how long she did this before he fell asleep again, but the next thing he remembered was hearing children's voices as they were laughing and playing. He opened his eyes to the dimness of an adobe room. What amazed him most was how comfortable the bed was, and he noticed that his pillow was feather-stuffed and covered with white linen. He rose to his elbows and studied the four-poster bed and the hand-sewn quilt that lay over him. Across from the bed was the door to the room, and it was closed. Next to the door was a chair, and folded on the chair were what appeared to be his clothes. Beside the bed was a stand made of the same wood as the bed, but he could not identify the type of wood because of its dark color. The stand was covered with a lace doily, and on the doily rested a porcelain washbasin.

He rose slowly from under the covers and realized he was naked. He wrapped himself with the quilt as he got out of the bed and walked toward the chair. Unlike most adobe structures Enrique had been in, this one had a wooden floor, and the planks creaked as he walked over them.

He picked up his clothes and studied how neatly they were folded. He set them on the floor, and as he sat naked in the chair he heard footsteps and suddenly the door opened. He fell startled to the floor and covered himself with the quilt again, then looked up into the face of the old woman.

"*Dios mía!* I am sorry, *señor!*" she said, backing out and quickly closing the door.

"Where in God's name am I?" Enrique said.

After he was dressed, he stepped over to a window and looked out into a court fenced by an adobe wall, and there played the children he had heard. There were four of them, all boys, and they played with toy guns and swords all made of wood. One of the boys fell, and the others took advantage and acted like they were annihilating him with their weapons. The make-believe victim did a fair job of imitating agony and death. It was disturbing to Enrique to think how, as children, they had likely never experienced real tragedy. For their sake, he hoped they never did.

He stepped out of his room and found himself on a railed balcony overlooking a dining room. Several servants, all Mexicans, walked about cleaning and preparing for a meal. He recognized the elderly woman who had tended to him, as she walked up the stairs toward him. Eventually she came up from the landing carrying fresh bed linen and smiled sheepishly at him.

"Good to see you are better, *señor*. You should come downstairs. Our *patrón* will want to see you."

Enrique ran his fingers through his hair and looked back down into the dining room. "Excuse me, *señora*, but where am I?"

"You are a guest at the rancho of Don Richard Benjamin."

He looked around the room again, then back at the woman. "But how did I get here?"

"Several of our *vaqueros* were out riding and they found you and your friends. They are all fine. But the young China girl is still very weak. Come. Follow me."

The woman set the linen down on a table and Enrique did as she asked. At the base of the stairs they went opposite to the dining room and down a long hall, sided with tall windows that displayed the court where the children played. Then, to their left was a den with a rectangular desk covered in leather. Sitting behind the desk was a sandy-haired gringo with long sideburns and a thick mustache. The mustache was darker than his other hair, with a hint of red, and it was waxed and curled upward on the ends. When they entered the room, he looked up at them with intense blue eyes and a friendly smile.

"Ah, I see you're up and at it," he said, standing. He walked out from behind the desk and shook Enrique's hand. "I am Dick Benjamin. Welcome to my ranch."

"*Gracias, Señor* Benjamin. I'm Enrique Osorio."

"Please, Enrique, call me Dick. And have a seat."

The rancher pointed a hand at a stuffed leather chair that matched the covering of his desk. He sat in a similar chair, only with a taller back.

"You folks were almost done in out there. Good thing my foreman ran into you. I've already met your sheriff friend. He's a little dried up and hungover from the sun, but he'll recover. Old cowboy, he says. He's out right now working with the *vaqueros*, waiting for you to get better."

"I appreciate your hospitality, Dick, but I am better and we must get going."

"Now, hold on to your breeches there, *amigo*. You need to eat a good meal before you take off. It's late afternoon. I'd appreciate it if you'd all be my guests for dinner tonight. Then, you can take off bright and early in the morning."

Enrique nodded slowly.

"And I know what you're after. You and every other bounty hunter that winds his way through this country."

"With all respect, *señor*, I am no bounty hunter."

"Yes, I know. Mr. Dutton explained everything to me. He also assured me there would be no stopping you. I admire a man with a mission, and I want to help."

"You've already been a great help, *señor*."

"Ah, but I can do better." The rancher opened a drawer on his desk and pulled out a Bible, not much bigger than his hand. He opened it and pulled out a photo that had been lodged between the pages. He handed the photo to Enrique. The *Criollo* was stunned by the beauty of the woman, with long, wavy brown hair and eyes like black beads.

"She and I were to be married. The day before our wedding she came up missing. I was afraid she'd gotten cold feet, then one of my *vaqueros* rode in with a broach that she had been wearing and a piece of her skirt that was torn."

"What happened to her?"

"Valdar."

Just like any other time, the sound of that name stabbed at every nerve in Enrique's body.

"He grabbed her while she was out riding. She must have been too hard for him to handle. She was a ball of fire, that woman. We found her two days later floating facedown in a creek. There was no doubt she'd been raped, and her throat was cut."

This was no surprise to Enrique. All he could do was nod and offer the photo back to the rancher.

"We tried going after him, but we lost his trail in Mexico. I've never gotten over it. But I'm too old to go after him. I have too much responsibility here. All these people depend on me, and I can't turn my back on them for something so personal."

"I understand, *señor.*" Enrique could see the hurt in the man's eyes, a hurt that he himself hadn't felt in years, and wondered how the man still felt it after all this time. All Enrique felt now was a steadfast hardness. He supposed the steadfastness came from his head; a feeling he'd grown accustomed to with his education and time with the priest. The hardness was a lock on his conscience, a way of pushing away sentiment for anything or anyone, regardless of how serious the pain. The priest had warned him about that feeling, that as a Christian he would have to open his heart to peace, grace, and forgiveness and allow God to carry the load of his difficult past. He supposed he had never really allowed that to happen. Maybe it was actually an attempt to be rid of the horror of it all rather than an acceptance of faith. Enrique wasn't sure, but he trusted Father Gaeta, so he supposed he trusted God. He just knew now that the path he had chosen was very clear to him, and that this rancher that stood before him needed justice, too, and Enrique wanted to help him.

"Whatever you need is yours," Benjamin said. "Clothes, food, weapons, horses—I'll make sure you're well equipped to make your journey to El Paso."

"I am very grateful."

"No, Enrique, I am grateful that the good Lord saw fit to lead you to me. Those bounty hunters that roll through here don't have the passion or grit to get the job done. They often find themselves on the other end of the knife and food for the buzzards. But I've seen what your Chinese friend can do. And the sheriff tells me you have a lot of savvy with a bow and arrow."

"*Señor,* would you happen to know of a mulberry tree on your *rancho*?"

The rancher wrinkled his forehead. "I'm sure we could find one. Why?"

"I prefer to use the wood to make my bow and arrows the Apache way."

Benjamin grinned and walked over to a glass gun cabinet at the side of the room, opened it, and produced a bow. He handed it to Enrique. "It was a gift to me from a Comanche friend. Never thought to use it; I kept it here as a reminder of what it took to get this land. I reckon it might need a new string, but it is my gift to you if you can use it."

Enrique studied the entire assembly carefully. "*Sí,* it is very authentic."

The rancher smiled. "I'm sure it is. My foreman can take you to find a tree to make your arrows. We have several on the ranch."

Enrique nodded as the rancher came from behind his desk, put a hand on Enrique's shoulder, and walked him through the house and out to the courtyard. The foreman, a *vaquero* of mature age, was close by, and he saddled a horse for the *Criollo.* Enrique had never been on a horse so tall. It was a bay with a black mane, and it seemed very gentle.

The *vaquero* spoke to him in Spanish. "She is an old mare and has lost a lot of her spirit. But she will take you where you want to go and will bring you home." He ended with a friendly smile.

"*Gracias,*" Enrique said.

\* \* \*

When Enrique entered the room, Pang was sitting in a chair beside the bed where Mun Lo lay sleeping. Pang acknowledged him somberly for only a second then turned his attention back to his sister.

The elderly woman walked in behind Enrique, carrying another stack of folded bed linen. She leaned over and saw that Mun Lo was sleeping. She smiled and whispered, "*Señorita?*"

Mun Lo's eyes opened slightly, and she looked up at the woman, then over at Pang. When she saw her brother, she smiled, but winced and brought a hand up to her chapped lips.

Chas Dutton walked in as well, and Enrique greeted him with a nod. "How's she doing?" Dutton said.

"She is weak," Pang said. "Too weak to travel."

"We can't afford to wait too long, Pang," Dutton said.

"We can't just leave her here."

The old woman dabbed a damp cloth on Mun Lo's lips. "She is in good hands here. You should go and do what you have to do."

Pang looked hard at Mun Lo, and she opened her eyes again and nodded her approval to him.

"I have gathered what I need to make more arrows," Enrique said. "We can leave in the morning."

Dutton grinned. "Ol' Benjamin gave me two Smith and Wesson .44s, a Henry rifle, and enough ammunition to take on Crook's army. I agree with Enrique, we should leave as soon as we can."

Pang looked back at his sister, grabbed her hand, then kissed her forehead. "I will be back for you."

* * *

That night the three men joined Benjamin and his foreman at his table, which held one of the biggest spreads of food Enrique had ever seen. The meal was served on silver, with a long platter holding four stuffed pheasants and beside the platter bowls of beans, squash, potatoes, and maize and three loaves of fresh baked bread. There was also a cloth towel on a plate that held warm tortillas. By each of their glass china plates were crystal goblets. A maid walked around the table and filled each goblet with a deep red wine. They were all dressed in new clothes, which Benjamin had also provided. Benjamin himself wore a black dress coat and a cravat, and his hair was slicked with tonic.

Once all the goblets were filled, Benjamin held his up and clanged it with a spoon. "I would like to toast your journey." Enrique and Pang, ignorant of this custom, slowly copied the other men's movements.

"To God and to passion," the rancher said. "May both be with you to the end."

All drank from their goblets. Enrique grimaced at the bitterness, as he had never tasted wine before, but he liked the warm feeling it suddenly gave him.

Benjamin prayed over the meal and they ate a great feast. Enrique could not recall ever having so much, or having food that tasted so good. Sure, part of that was hunger, but the food was still immaculately prepared. Not the priest, or even his mother, had ever prepared such a grand meal.

Enrique could not remember a morning where he had felt so much at peace, or such unwavering confidence. Like any normal man, he at first questioned how he could have such a feeling. Just like the horses that Benjamin had given them, and the many supplies, weapons, and foodstuffs, the feeling was overwhelmingly abundant. They were making a new start on this journey better equipped than they had ever been.

Pang had his normal morning routine in the wilderness, with breathing and stretching exercises, and when he was done, he spent a few minutes saying good-bye to Mun Lo. Dutton wasted no time preparing his horse and packing his goods, and while he waited on the others, he watched a young *vaquero* train a horse.

Just as the sun made its appearance, Benjamin came out on the front porch of his ranch home and into the courtyard. His foreman stood at his side, and all of the maids and servants behind him. Benjamin shook each of their hands, and when he shook Enrique's, he grabbed it with the other hand as well and held it tight. "I'll be praying for you, son."

Enrique nodded and tipped his hat to all the servants, then mounted his horse. It was not the same bay mare that he'd ridden the day before, but a younger sorrel that the foreman said would handle the trail and the chase.

He nudged it forward, and the others followed. He wasn't sure how long it would be before they picked up Valdar's trail, but it really didn't matter. All he knew was that once the horses were warm they would lope until they found it, and until then all they had to do was head southeast. Southeast to El Paso.

# MULCOV THE RUSSIAN

All the years that Enrique had dreamed about this journey he had always envisioned it being with his grandfather. The details were simple; they would ride out, find Valdar and the renegades, see them, kill them, and all would be over. But now the harsh reality of the pursuit had set in. Ever since they left the mission, there had been obstacles, both human and natural, that interfered and challenged the will to carry on. Enrique was thankful for the wisdom of the priest, who'd taught him about the need for patience. If not for the priest, Enrique would have often been impulsive and not waited for the right moment. This was proven true when Pang came into his life, and when they met Sheriff Dutton, Geronimo, and the good rancher Don Benjamin.

Enrique nosed the sorrel dead east now. He looked back occasionally to check on his friends. How different they all looked now. Dutton stayed with his Anglo cowboy gear—a felt hat, placket shirt and neckerchief, and chaps for the brush. Pang wore the clothes of a Mexican—a wide sombrero and a waist-length *chaqueta* with matching *pantalones*, the cuffs tucked inside his knee-high boots. Though he also wore a sombrero, Enrique stuck with his traditional *serape* and cotton *pantalones*.

They came to a knoll dotted with barrel cactus, yucca, agave, and fluff grass, around which a trail led to a lowland stream. The horses could smell the water, and the sorrel tried to pick up its pace, but Enrique would not enter a foreign area too swiftly, especially one of higher and greener grasses, with contents below unknown.

They found a bend in the stream where the water pooled, and figured it to be the best place to let the horses drink and to fill their canteens. Enrique checked the water first to make sure it wasn't poisoned with alkali, and nodded to the others to bring the horses ahead.

Once they had had their fill and a good rest, they continued on for more than three hours following the stream, which meandered south; then they found the trail to Hachita that Don Benjamin had told them about. It was a trail first made by Spaniards and kept in use by ranchers and miners and now mostly the people of Hachita. It was a trail that Valdar wouldn't take, but a good one for them to gain ground and a better chance at meeting him in El Paso.

Dusk was upon them, and Enrique mentioned the idea of camping for the night.

"Good idea," Dutton said, already dismounting. "Always good to camp near water in these parts."

Pang, the tireless one, stayed mounted and peered east down the trail. Enrique patted him lightly on the knee. "I know, *mi amigo*. We will start out again bright and early."

"There is still an hour of daylight. We could get that much further at least."

"In this land we cannot deny the gift of water. We must take advantage of it. Who knows when we will find it again?"

Pang kept looking down the trail, but he gave in to the wisdom of his friend and dismounted. He gave the reins to Dutton, who took both horses to a mesquite bush and tied them up. He unsaddled Pang's horse for him, too, since the Chinaman never seemed to catch on when it came to gearing up or gearing down his mount.

After unsaddling his horse and giving it some grain, Enrique walked down to the stream with his canteen in hand. He knelt before the shore, laid his sombrero down, pulled the cap, and dipped the canteen into the cool, glistening water. He adored the sound of rippling water, and it brought back several memories of his life along the Santa Cruz, during those first few days following a rain. He listened closely, watching the motions of the current and the cascading light, offering back his own distorted reflection. Such moments of peace seemed few as he grew older, and he wondered why. He could almost hear the laughing voices of children playing in the water, like the ones near Tucson. As he smiled at the thought, he suddenly realized that he wasn't imagining those voices.

He stood slowly, looked across the river, and saw movement. A smile came to his face when he saw Sereno, but then he noticed that Sereno had a serious look about him and quickly vanished.

He heard the voices again and looked farther down-stream, but he saw nothing humanlike that could make such sounds. He capped the canteen and walked along the shore. He came to a bend with rich grama grasses and reeds as tall as his chin. As he peered around the bend, the voices of laughter grew louder, and their source came vividly into view and froze Enrique without a breath.

They were his age, he supposed, standing thigh-deep in the water washing each other, laughing and sharing conversation. One stood behind the other, cupping her hands and lifting water up on the other's back and shoulders. The other washed her own front by reaching down and lifting water to pour over her head, face, and breasts.

Enrique had rarely thought about women sexually, and when he did it was usually during trips to Tucson with the priest. The priest would warn him to be cautious of the girls in the city. They would lure you into a trap and you'd find yourself without a heart or a home. He trusted the priest completely, and he did as he said, but it still didn't stop him from looking. Point was, this was the first time he'd ever seen women naked.

They weren't particularly pretty, like some of the women he'd seen. The one behind stood a good three inches taller than the other, and she was slender and very dark-skinned. Her long black hair was slick and wet and draped over her shoulder, partially covering her breasts. The other was more voluptuous with larger breasts and hips, and her skin and hair lighter like that of an Anglo.

Enrique was not sure what to do at the moment, but his natural male curiosity drove him to get closer for a better look. He stepped back into the grass and hunched low as he crept forward. The coolness of the water seeped in through the soles of his boots. He took several steps, hearing their voices grow louder and louder, and he could faintly see them through the reeds.

He came to a point where he thought he was close enough and parted the reeds with both hands for a better look. But what he saw most of was not the women, but the long neck of a blue heron, which after it saw him, leapt into the air and whisked its wings into an alarming flight. Enrique fell backward, making a loud splash into the water, and the laughing voices of the women ceased.

"*Dios mío!*" Enrique said, under his breath, his buttocks and elbows deep under the water.

He decided to try and crawl out, and as he rolled around, a water snake slithered through the grass near his arm. He stood abruptly and yelled, but the harmless snake, as scared as he was, headed out to the stream.

His alarm became their alarm, and the women screamed at his sight, covering their breasts and high-stepping out of the stream. When they made it to shore, they ran faster away from him, toward a lean-to shelter farther upstream.

When they left his view, Enrique could hear their frightened voices, and suddenly another figure appeared. He was a large, pale man with a completely bald head, large bushy eyebrows, and wearing a long white cotton robe and thong sandals. He marched downstream in long strides, head high pursuant to whatever the women had reported to him.

Enrique still stood, as frozen as he was when he had first seen the women, yet now dripping wet and afraid in a peculiar sort of way.

"Who goes there?" the man shouted from across the stream.

Enrique could not gather the words to respond.

"Who are you and what is your business?"

"I am sorry, *señor*. I didn't mean to frighten anyone. I was just filling my canteen."

The man got as close as he could without getting into the water and studied Enrique with ice-blue eyes. "Ah, a Mexican. And a wet one at that. Besides filling your canteen, what is your business near my river?"

"I am Tohono O'odham, not Mexican, and I am traveling, *señor*. To El Paso, with two others. They are behind me on the trail."

The man's intent eyes never blinked. "El Paso, eh?"

*"Sí, señor."*

Suddenly and without warning the man smiled and belched a hearty laugh. "I guess you filled your eyes as well as your canteen, eh, *Papago*?"

Enrique looked away, embarrassed.

"Come," the man said, waving his arm. "Take a break from your travels and join me for supper. Bring your friends!"

Enrique could hardly turn him down, but he feared the embarrassment he would feel seeing the women again. He supposed that his embarrassment was just punishment for his lust. The priest had warned him about it, but at least all he did was look. Touching the premarital flesh was something that the priest warned would bring dire consequences, and something Enrique was certain he would not do.

Dutton liked the idea of a hot meal and agreed to the

invitation, and though cautious, Pang made no objection as well. Enrique thought it best not to mention what had happened with the women, mostly out of fear of what kind of questions they would ask him.

The men took their horses and gear across the stream to the canvas lean-to and were greeted by a jovial host. A dozen chickens, ducks, and geese walked about near the dwelling.

"Ah, we have a trio of trailblazers! Welcome! Welcome to my humble home!"

Dutton walked up close to Enrique and whispered in his ear. "For a fat feller he's sure got a lot of fire under his robe."

Enrique sighed and continued on.

"My name is Mulcov," the man said. Almost every time he talked, he ended with a laugh. Sometimes a little chuckle, other times with one all the way from the bottom of his big stomach.

Enrique introduced his companions and himself.

"Such a variety you are! Come, come inside and rest your weary feet."

The lean-to leaned against a large, rocky mass that jutted out from a hill next to the stream. Enrique had seen his share of such dwellings, but none this large. It was as wide as the nave of the mission and half as long. White canvas made the roof and sides and was rolled up in the front and tied off. A rug covered most of the floor area, the rest pruned of all vegetation and brushed clean with a broom. A rough-hewn table stood near a center support pole made of pine from the mountains. A lantern hung on the pole, shedding just enough light to attract biting insects. Mulcov lit several candles. Enrique kept looking around for the women.

Mulcov asked the visitors to sit. Several empty wooden kegs were positioned upside down around the table. Their host sat with them on the end and rubbed his hands together vigorously, his blue eyes gleaming.

He raised his hands and clapped them twice loudly. "Woman! Bring us drink!"

In walked the shorter of the two women. Dutton quickly removed his hat and rose from his seat. Enrique swallowed and fidgeted on his. At least she wasn't naked this time. Now she wore a *huipil* and moccasins. The woman set a clear bottle on the table, with a label printed in a language Enrique had never seen. She opened a trunk and pulled out four glass goblets and brought them to the table as well. She made no eye contact with any of them. Not even Mulcov.

"Now, go bring the tamales. *Andale!*" Mulcov shooed her away with his hand, then looked to his guests with a broad smile. "Ah, it's so nice to have guests!" he said, pouring them each a drink and setting the goblets in front of them. "I am so happy that I will share with you my best vodka from the home country. And my favorite tamales, like they make in the Yucatan."

After all the drinks were poured, Mulcov held his head up high. "As they say here in the Americas, *salud!*"

He didn't wait on them, but drank all of his in one swallow. Dutton tipped his back confidently and after swallowing stretched his mouth and wiped his lips with his fingers.

Pang lifted his goblet slowly and sniffed. He turned up his nose and peered at Enrique. Enrique shrugged and looked down into the glass.

"Bottoms up, lads!" Mulcov shouted. "Drink like that shapes the man and stirs the gods!"

Enrique took a large swallow and came back choking. Pang tried his as well, with similar results.

All the drama drew a belly laugh from Mulcov. "It gets better, gentlemen. The tamales will be made special for you tonight, with sweet brown beans and corn and, as a treat, *pollo.*"

Enrique liked tamales, but he hadn't had them in years. It was a traditional food made mostly by the people of the Mayan culture, but passed on to the Mexican generations as well. He wasn't sure how different tamales from the Yucatán would be, but when the slender young woman, also wearing a *huipil*, came in with them steaming on a tray, he realized that they were much larger than any tamale he'd ever seen.

"Ah, how grand!" Mulcov said, unwrapping the corn husks and diving right in.

Enrique made the cross over his chest, then took a tamale from the tray. He untied the corn husk and unfolded it. They were prepared beautifully and tasted just as good as they looked. The woman who'd prepared them knew what she was doing.

"So," Mulcov said, "you all are heading to *Paso del Norte.* What is the attraction of that fine city?"

The three men exchanged glances, Pang still blinking his watery eyes from his big swallow of vodka.

Dutton decided to answer for them. "We have business there. We need to get there quickly, but our horses need a rest."

"And so do you, my friends!" Mulcov raised his glass again. "To your journey!"

Enrique dreaded the idea of taking another drink, and apparently Pang felt the same and saw fit to knock over his glass, the contents pooling and quickly absorbing into the dry wood of the tabletop.

"No worries, my friend," Mulcov said. "We have more." Mulcov grabbed the bottle, but Pang picked up his goblet and placed his hand over the top.

"No, thank you," Pang said.

It was the most solemn look Enrique had seen on Mulcov since they met at the stream.

Dutton decided to change the subject. "Quite a setup you have here, Mulcov."

A smile came back to him. "Ah, yes, this is my paradise."

"Ain't none of my business," Dutton said, "but I'm just curious, how a big ol' boy like you makes a living out here in the wilderness. Just you and two little Indian gals."

Mulcov smiled proudly. "I left Russia with much money, and came to the Americas to start a new life. I spend many years in Mexico, doing business with the *federales*, but now I retire to a life of leisure."

Dutton grinned. "And them Indian girls, I reckon they're part of that leisure?"

"Ah yes, Mr. Dutton. They are not my wives, but better than wives! They cook and clean for me . . ." The Russian leaned forward. "And other things, too, if you know what I mean."

The laughed that followed, Enrique was certain, could be heard all the way to El Paso.

"Kind of dangerous out here, just you and the women," Enrique said.

"Mulcov is afraid of no one!"

"Not even Antonio Valdar?" Enrique said.

"Ah, the Demon Warrior. No, he will not harm me. We made many treaties in Mexico."

"You have a treaty with Valdar?"

"Of course! He is the source of my two women. He would not harm a good customer, would he?"

The three men exchanged glances.

Enrique developed a sudden distaste for their host. "If you will excuse me, *señor*, I am tired and wish to get some sleep. Thank you for the invitation."

Mulcov watched the *Criollo* stand and walk out of the lean-to without saying a word. Pang immediately followed and caught up with Enrique.

"What did I say?" the Russian said.

Dutton slid down the last of his vodka and pushed the empty goblet toward Mulcov. "You seem like the harmless type, so I'll fill you in so there's no hurt feelings."

"Harmless? Of course, I would not harm a bug."

"Those two men out there lost their families because of Valdar. Their women were abducted to be taken to Mexico and sold. You are the end result of exactly what we're going to El Paso to stop."

Mulcov stared at the table and furrowed his brow. "I see. But I mean no harm to my women. They have a good life."

Dutton stood on his feet. "They are your slave girls and you know it. Someone somewhere cries for them, but I doubt that matters much to you. So long as you get your vodka and meals on time, and a little wilderness poke when you so desire."

The Russian slammed a fist on the table. "I am doing nothing wrong! I've broken no laws!"

"I'm not putting you on trial here, Mulcov. You're just the pitiful end to a heinous crime. And there ain't enough paper in the world to write all the laws that would cover a good healthy conscience."

"I will ask you to leave here, Mr. Dutton. Take your friends and go."

Dutton grabbed his hat and headed out of the lean-to. He stopped and turned his head back. "One more thing. If you think for one minute that Valdar respects any man, you're fooling yourself more than anyone. You better dread the day he returns here and decides he wants the women back. And I can promise you he won't be payin' cash for them, or respecting any so-called treaty."

The trio made camp a good twenty yards from the stream, laying out their bedrolls and building a fire for warmth and morning coffee. Enrique and Pang had spoken little since they'd left the Russian's lean-to, but they had exchanged many glances, which were enough for them to know they both felt the same desire.

Dutton settled in beside the fire and spoke of the unusual silence among them. "You boys need to let that all go and not get in the way of what we have to do."

Enrique only looked at him.

"I know what you're thinking," Dutton said. "It's not healthy, Enrique."

"The only difference between those *mujeres* and *mi hermana*, and Pang's fiancée, is that they are not ours. But they are somebody's children. Someone's daughter, someone's sister, maybe even someone's wife. I will not be able to live with myself riding away from here without helping them."

"How do you know they want to be helped?" Dutton asked.

Enrique exchanged a look of frustration with Pang then stood up from his bedroll. He spat into the fire and gave Dutton a hard stare. "You go to sleep, Sheriff, and sleep well if you can. I'm going to rescue those women and see that they get back home to their families. If you want to stop me, I suggest you try now."

Pang rose quickly to his feet. "I'm going with you."

Enrique and Pang crossed the stream and snuck into the Russian's camp. The canvas in the front had been rolled down and a faint light glowed from the inside. Enrique wasn't sure where the women stayed, but it was a good bet that they were in there with the Russian.

Pang went around to the back side with a plan to sneak in between the canvas and the rock. He didn't carry a weapon; he didn't need one. His mind was always his best weapon.

Enrique went to the front, giving Pang enough time to work his way in, and then flipped up the canvas. He fully expected to find them all sleeping, and he would wake them, overpower the Russian, and free the women. But never in his life did he expect to see them all awake; the big Russian sat on a barrel with nothing on but a linen wrap around his waist. His large, portly, ashen body glistened under the lantern light. The taller woman stood behind Mulcov, rubbing oil on his shoulders. The other woman sat on the rug in front of him washing his feet. The Russian raised his nose in the air and moaned, occassionaly mumbling the words "yes" and "wonderful."

Enrique did not look long before the woman behind Mulcov noticed him and shrieked loudly. Mulcov's eyes opened and he jerked his head sideways. He looked to see what had frightened the woman. She stood behind him now, making sure her *huipil* was closed tightly.

"What the hell!" Mulcov shouted.

He stood and walked away from the other woman, and she rose and joined the taller woman behind Mulcov. The Russian just stood there glaring, his oily body glistening under the lamplight. He held out his arms as if protecting the women.

"I am here to free them," Enrique said. "*Mujeres*, you are free to go as you please."

They did not move.

"Like hell," Mulcov said. "Who the hell do you think you are?" By this time he was growling, arms arched at his sides like a hairless grizzly bear. He charged Enrique and tackled him to the ground. The weight of the man on top of him made it difficult for him to breathe, and Enrique could not move him. It got worse when Mulcov brought a forearm up and laid it over his throat and pushed down with all his weight. Enrique could feel the blood compressing in his skull and his very life vanishing before him.

Pang jumped in on top of Mulcov, but not even the swift moves of martial arts could penetrate the stout layers of this bear of a man. But a sudden noise made everything stop. It was the click of a revolver. Mulcov stopped growling, and the pressure from his arm slowly lifted off Enrique's neck. Enrique gasped and choked. Pang backed away. Mulcov rose slowly with a barrel of a gun pressed firmly against his forehead.

As soon as he could, Enrique choked and crawled out, and watched Sheriff Dutton coax Mulcov to his feet and to the back of the lean-to.

"You're making a big mistake," Mulcov said.

"I beg to differ," Dutton said. "If your brains end up splattered on that rock wall behind you, then who's mistake will it be?"

Dutton glanced over at Enrique. "All right, you got what you wanted. Get them dressed and get them out of here."

Enrique nodded and spoke Spanish to the women. They both hunched together and shook their heads.

"It's okay," he said. "We're here to help you. You can go home now."

"We have no other home," the slender one said. "Our families are dead."

"Then you are free now. You can do whatever you want with your lives."

"And do what? We are unclean. Who will accept us?"

"You are God's children. Do good and you will find your place in this world."

The shorter one shook her head. "Our place is here. Mulcov will take care of us."

Enrique was dumbfounded. Dutton was right. They had all risked their lives to save them, yet they didn't want to be saved.

"See, I told you," Mulcov said. "You made a mistake."

Dutton lowered his revolver and Mulcov seemed to breathe a little easier.

"There's one other thing," Dutton said to the women. "We aim to kill Valdar. But if we don't, he'll likely find you again. Don't think for one minute that Mulcov can save you from him."

They both stared intently, and the slender one raised her head. "Then you must kill him."

There was no convincing them, and Enrique ran out of the lean-to. He had never considered what such a change in their lives would do to them. He thought of his own sister, and if she was still alive, whether or not she would be able to return to a happier life. It was a new and sad reality. One that would take some time to set in.

# THE HACHITA TRAIL

By noon the next day they rode into the settlement of Hachita, watered and grained their horses, and Sheriff Dutton nosed out a small adobe *taberna*. They tied their horses to a hitching rail and Dutton led the way inside.

Pang took the rear, and before entering he stressed his concern. "Shouldn't someone stay with the horses?"

Dutton looked back. "We'll only be a minute. Lube our tonsils, ask a couple of questions, then be back on our way."

"But he is right," Enrique said. "We've lost everything once. We may not find it all again."

"I will stay with them," Pang said.

Dutton shrugged. "Suit yourself. I'm thirsty."

The sheriff turned, and Enrique followed, and they walked out of the bright day and into the darkness of a room with the only light source a few oil lamps that hung randomly on each wall and beams of light that seeped down through gaps in the thatch above. When their eyes had adjusted, they found two tables, one occupied by an old Mexican nursing a drink and the other table empty. An Anglo, middle-aged and with a full salt-and-pepper beard, stood behind a bar wiping a glass. He wore a cotton shirt and his face perspired. In a far corner of the room a Mexican man sat in a chair playing a guitar. A sombrero hung on his back by the chin chord. A young, barefoot Mexican woman in a long red-and-yellow dress danced and twirled to his Spanish music.

Dutton walked up to the bar with more confidence than Enrique. "What do you serve in here, barkeep?"

The bartender eyeballed them both. "*Cerveza*. Tequila. Mescal. No whiskey."

"Should have known." Dutton flipped out a couple of coins on the bar, part of some expense money given to them by Benjamin, which could also be used to buy information. One coin was more than enough for the two beers Dutton ordered, and he figured the bartender would catch his drift. Judging by the way the bartender looked at the coins, as if they were something dangerous, and swiftly slid them off into his hand and into his pocket, Dutton had assumed right.

The bartender slapped two beers down on the bar, both frothing over. Dutton slid one down in front of Enrique then took a drink from his own. He smacked his lips and studied the dark amber color through the glass. "You Mexicans sure know how to brew. But different than that ol' German beer I'm used to."

Enrique reflected back to the vodka and wasn't too excited about trying the beer. The priest had discouraged him from drinking, except for medicinal purposes. The father had showed him passages in the Bible that mentioned drinking but chastised drunkenness, and told him how Enrique's own drinking could "cause his brother to stumble." He assured him that a single drink would not curse his soul to hell, but avoiding it altogether was the best way to not go too far.

Enrique looked around the bar and didn't see any men who would stumble any farther than they already had, and he knew he wouldn't be in the bar long enough to find drunkenness, so he declared to himself that having a beer with the sheriff was no signature sin.

The first sip wasn't as biting as the vodka, or the wine, but it had a different bitterness to his still very virgin tongue. He decided to take another, bigger drink, then somewhat held his breath and swallowed twice. It was hard not to gag, but he kept drinking in that fashion until suddenly the brew went down much better and almost became refreshing. It was an interesting contrast, he thought, and the priest's teaching made some sense. He had said, "When first drawn to the temptation of sin, it is very uncomfortable. But when the line keeps being crossed, the devil shows you pleasure and tries to make his snag."

Dutton finished his beer and slid the glass to the edge. The bartender came forward, now trying not to look Dutton in the eye. *"Mas?"*

"No," Dutton said. "But I'd like to finish out my credit."

The bartender looked around the room nervously. The music seemed to get louder, and the woman moved her feet faster to the tempo.

"We're after Antonio Valdar," Dutton said. "I know you know who he is. I just want to know if he's been through here recently."

The bartender shook his head. "I didn't see him."

Dutton flipped another coin on the bar. The bartender swiped it up quicker than the last ones.

"Two days ago. Outside of town. But he didn't stay long."

"He have anyone with him?"

He looked around the room again, and over Dutton's shoulder. "I don't remember seeing anyone else."

Dutton wrinkled his mouth and frustratingly threw out another coin.

"He had one Apache. And he had several horses."

Dutton and Enrique exchanged glances. Enrique was a little more at ease knowing they were on the right trail, but not as confident knowing Valdar had a two-day gap on them.

The two of them turned around to leave, and a Mexican man walked in the main door. Immediately following him was a younger Mexican sporting a rifle. Compared to most in this small settlement, these two were clearly better off, judging by the way they dressed. Both wore new trousers and snow-white shirts, and the older man wore a vest. Near the placket of that vest was a badge.

Dutton and Enrique headed for the door, but the constable didn't move to let them through.

"*Con permiso*," Dutton said.

"In my town, a man leaves when I say."

Dutton stared the man down. The young man behind him ran the lever action on the rifle and offered the same cold, blank stare.

"Don't be in such a hurry, *señor*," the lawman said. He pointed a hand at the empty table. "Let me buy you a drink."

Dutton contemplated a fight, but decided he didn't have enough information on this man's intentions to start one. It was worth a chance to find out first whose side he was on, even though Dutton was pretty sure he already knew.

Dutton turned slowly toward the table and took a chair. Enrique followed, as did the constable, but the deputy with the rifle stayed by the door.

The constable sat with his belly against the table and his elbows on it. Dutton scooted away, his holstered revolver in clear view of all of them, something he wanted them to see. Besides, he'd witnessed enough under-the-table shootings in bars to know a man had a much better chance if he could see beneath the table.

"*Señor*, I am Juan Ortega. I am the *policía* here. When strangers come into town, I must know their business. Especially ones with Chinamen."

"What about Chinawomen? When someone comes through town with one of them, do you ask their business?"

Ortega stared.

Dutton nodded. "That's what I thought. We can cut through the sheep dip here pretty quickly, *patrón*. Just tell me whose payroll you're on, and I'll know whether or not we'll have to fight to get out of here."

The constable frowned. "I see you have little respect for men of authority."

"The only authority on me is the man upstairs. Now which is it? You work for the people or Valdar?"

Dutton already knew, simply by the way the constable dressed, but he could tell more by the contempt in Ortega's eyes that the latter was definitely the correct answer. It also confirmed that there'd be no way out without a fight.

"You will have to come with me, *señor*," Ortega said. "You may try to stop me with that iron at your side, but before your arm is bent to grab it, my deputy will have put a bullet hole through your thick gringo skull."

Dutton glanced at the deputy, who was definitely ready to do just as Ortega said.

"Afraid I can't go along with your plan," Dutton said. "I'll have to take my chances. The first move is yours."

Ortega's frown never changed. The guitar music that had once been soft and refreshing seemed to keep growing louder and faster, and the dancing girl kept her twirl with the pace.

Just as Dutton was contemplating what his move would be, a large ruckus came from outside the door. The deputy glanced nervously back and forth, then in walked Pang, arms hanging wide and head turning in all directions. Once he saw the deputy with the gun, he threw a forearm up against the barrel of the rifle. The gun went off, shooting a dusty hole in the adobe wall, and about the same time Pang's foot came around and kidney-kicked the deputy to the floor.

The music stopped, as did the dancing girl.

Ortega had turned his head during the gun blast, and before he could turn it back around, Dutton's fist caught his right temple and sent him fumbling out of the chair. He was out cold.

A shotgun blast was the next diversion. Dutton was glad to know it was the thatch roof that took the buckshot, redirected by Enrique's knife stuck in the bartender's chest.

Dutton drew his gun and turned quickly toward the guitar player and dancer. The man still sat, his hands over the guitar and motionless. The woman stood with her hands wide at her side, her mouth agape and her black eyes full of fear.

Dutton holstered his gun then looked at Enrique, who had retrieved his knife. "I didn't know you could throw a knife like that."

Enrique smiled. "Neither did I, really. I just had to pretend he was a saguaro back by the Santa Cruz."

"Damn glad it worked."

"That makes two of us."

When the three men walked out of the *taberna* and into the daylight, they stumbled over three men who lay unconscious on the dusty ground, their rifles next to them.

"What the hell?" Dutton said. He turned to Pang.

The Chinaman grinned. "They insisted they had me outnumbered."

Dutton shook his head and patted Pang on the shoulder. "You are some *hombre*."

The trio rode out of town with just a little more than they rode in with. They now knew what they needed to know about Valdar, and they knew they needed to pick up their pace to catch him before he left El Paso. Traveling in the territory, and battling the natural and social elements there, was one thing, but doing the same in Mexico was a much different game. The country was much more primitive, and the sight of gringo travelers—especially with a Chinaman— was more apt to land them in prison than anywhere else, or working for some greedy *patrón* in his quest for money and power.

That whole scenario had been a concern to Enrique as much as to Dutton. But one thing that was new to Enrique was the money he now knew that Dutton carried. They rode for almost an hour before he drummed up the courage to ask him.

"Where did you get it?" he asked.

Dutton turned his head and his brow furrowed. His shoulders tipped back and forth to the horse's footing. "Get what?"

"The money. You lost all you had to Valdar, and neither Pang nor I had any."

"Benjamin gave it to me. He knew you wouldn't accept it."

"He was right. It is my pleasure to kill Valdar. Money will not make me want it any more."

"It's not that, Enrique. Benjamin knew we'd need some to buy more supplies and maybe information. Though you might consider it a bounty, I think of it more as expense money. Benjamin just wanted to help out. Hell, it's no different than that horse you're riding or the saddle you're sitting in. It's all to help get the job done."

Enrique looked straight ahead. The sheriff was convincing. Father Gaeta had warned Enrique of the temptations of money, and how greed could bury a man's soul in hell, but this seemed like nothing that could harm them. Besides, the money was in the hands of the sheriff. Enrique had nothing to do with it.

"How much did he give you?" Enrique said.

"Fifty dollars in silver. It's not a lot by any means, but enough to get us through the ordeal."

Enrique nodded. "I suppose."

"You know, Enrique, money is not a bad thing."

"I have survived just fine without it."

"But there'll be a day when you can't."

"I don't see how. I can hunt game to eat. And I can build

my shelter from the gifts of the land as well. If I need clothes, I can trade for them. I have done it all my life."

"I understand that. But something you don't know is that my race of people intends to change all that. They may not realize it, and that's the sad part. But more and more of them are coming to this part of the country, and all the game and timber in the mountains won't last ten years. They already did it to the buffalo and deer on the upper plains. It's only a matter of time before it happens here."

"Then how will they survive? What good is money if there is nothing to buy?"

"It's called the railroad. Them iron rails is like the new bloodline that feeds the West. Boxcars full of livestock going back east to slaughter, and banks here to put all that cattle money in. And when the trains come back west, they bring goods ready to use. They hang 'em up on a wall or put 'em on a shelf in a mercantile and all you need is money."

To Enrique it sounded like a strange fantasy, but he'd seen it going on in Tucson, which was enough for him to believe it. "This money, how will we get it?"

"You find yourself a trade, Enrique. Something that you enjoy doing. Something that you're good at."

"I'm not sure what I would do. All I've ever been good at is hunting and living off the land."

"You can read and write, can't you?"

"Yes. Father Gaeta educated me well."

"That's a hell lot more than I have. You're a good fighter. Good with a bow and arrow. You can throw a knife. You might just make a good lawman."

Enrique shook his head. "I know a little about politics, and that is something I would not like."

Dutton laughed. "You got me there. That is definitely the fly in the buttermilk. Always something getting in the way of doing your job the right way, or even enjoying it at all."

They rode for a little while in silence, pondering all that had been shared.

"This way of life that you say is coming," Enrique said, "I'm not sure I want it."

"Don't think you'll have much choice, pardner. I suppose you could go live in the hills and fend for yourself, but what kind of life is that?"

Enrique nodded. "It may be the life for me. I'm not sure."

"Then I suppose you have a lot to think about."

"Yes," he said. *And more than I'd like right now*, he thought.

# PASO DEL NORTE

The three riders pushed the horses as much as they could. Dutton, the better and more experienced rider, knew exactly when to give the animals a rest. He'd look for lather around the rigging strap and watch carefully for rocks and cactuses along the trail that might lame a horse.

Whenever he suggested a break, Enrique went along with his advice, fully trusting the sheriff's expertise in the matter. Pang, however, never hesitated to question his decision.

"We should keep going," Pang said. "The more we stop, the farther Valdar gets away from us."

Dutton looked at the Chinaman under the shade of his hat brim. "You push these horses too much and you'll be walking after Valdar. Just how much quicker you think you'd gain on him then?"

As always when they stopped, Pang gazed off into the

distance, then frustratingly got down and handed the sheriff his reins.

Dutton took them hesitantly. "One of these days I'm going to have to teach you how to tear down your own horse."

Pang just kept walking.

Enrique stood next to Dutton and watched the Chinaman with him. "He's still fresh in his misery. I'd be the same way."

"Yeah, I forget about that sometimes," Dutton said.

They decided to let the horses rest for an hour, then they'd take off again. Meanwhile, Enrique found Pang, his arms around his knees, perched up on a big rock staring down into a lush valley near the base of the Florida Mountains. Enrique felt a desire to console his friend and allow him the opportunity to get his frustration out. He climbed up the rock, sat down beside Pang, and gazed out to the valley that he knew was just a haze among all of the Chinaman's thoughts.

"I love this country," Enrique said. "The sheriff tells me that its natural state is facing its doom."

"We are all doomed to something," Pang said. "The good times fade to memories, and life never seems to be as good as it once was."

Though Pang was likely feeling philosophical, Enrique could sense the Chinaman's self-pity. "Not long after my parents were killed, Father Gaeta told me that I had to stop living for tomorrow and live for today. It took me a while to understand what he meant, but eventually it came to me. I lived every day as though it was a step to the moment I sought my revenge against Valdar. I didn't realize I was missing out on an important learning time. A time of preparation. Important time when learning to become a man. The priest instilled in me how living one day at a time required a daily routine of appreciating what God had given me. The sunrise and the morning air. The birds and how they sang. The food in front of me, and how to chew and taste each bite as if it was all I would eat the entire day, or not knowing whether or not it'd be my last meal. From this thinking came patience, and faith."

Pang turned and looked at him. "But now you are going after Valdar. How can you think of anything else?"

"It is the purpose of each day, yes . . . to get a little closer to him. But I still stop and admire what God has given me. Such as you and *Señor* Dutton. Together we are much stronger."

Pang broke a slight smile. "You talk a lot like my father did. He was always trying to get me to breathe more, think less. He liked to call me a grasshopper." He breathed in and out deeply. "You are wise like him."

"I am only wise to the teachings of Father Gaeta, and what I've learned through reading the Scriptures and other books."

Pang nodded. "I think it is no chance that we met in the desert. I think it was destiny."

Enrique laughed. "I knew that the minute you first said Valdar's name, *amigo*. I try not to be overconfident in our purpose, and be humble as well, but deep in my heart I believe that together we are the ones who can bring Valdar's evil existence to an end."

"What about the sheriff?" Pang said. "Why is he with us?"

"It is not hard, once you think about it. Look at all that he has done for us. He has negotiated and used his lawman experience to help us get this far. Who knows what would have happened to us if he hadn't of helped us at the *taberna*, or put his gun to Mulcov's big bald head."

Pang smiled wider than he had in some time. "I've never tried to handle a man so big before. When I jumped on him, it was like trying to wrestle a bull."

Enrique laughed. "I knew I was in trouble when you couldn't budge him. Thank God for the sheriff's change of heart."

"Why do you suppose he didn't want to help us at first?"

"I think it was because he doesn't have our history, or our misery. I think he came to help us because of one reason, and one reason only."

"What is that?"

"Because we are his friends."


To make better time the riders took shorter breaks to rest the horses and rode also during the night. It was an easier decision because of the full moon, which shed just enough light across the landscape to stay on the trails. Dutton led the way and used the stars to navigate, the Big Dipper and the North Star.

Pang wasn't fond of the nocturnal voices of the wilderness, and he shifted nervously in his saddle, frequently asking Enrique to identify the creature that made a particular noise. The crickets and locusts he understood, but the owl he was unfamiliar with and he cared little for the coyote. What made him fidget the most, however, was when he noticed the silhouette of a wing span flutter in front of the moon.

"What was that?" he said.

"The most worrisome creature of the night," Enrique said. "The blood-sucking bat is attracted to the scent of sweat, and in humans the salt of the neck."

Pang kept looking up at the moon, and when two more flew across its light, the Chinaman lifted up his collar and hunched his neck.

Enrique laughed. "I'm only joking with you, *amigo*. The bat is after flying insects. It cannot see, but can sense them uniquely. It will not harm you."

Pang was not amused, and Enrique's admission of the truth had made him no more at ease.

They rode for another hour, and the night sky began to turn from a deep purple to more of a deep blue, and the moon disappeared behind a cloud low in the western sky. The stars still twinkled, but not for long, as daylight fast approached. Dutton figured they were a six-hour ride from El Paso and that this would be a good time to rest and eat.

Enrique decided not to build a fire and supplied jerky and corn tortillas for breakfast. They drank from their canteens and hoped they'd soon find water for their horses. The grain that Benjamin had given them was almost gone as well, but it was enough to last until they reached El Paso.

Little was said while they ate and rested. Their horses stood behind them, reins hanging loose, eyes closed, and one hind leg cocked at the fetlock.

Dutton was the first to finish eating. "Well, boys, I suppose it's time to roam."

Pang shoved what was left of his jerky to the side of his mouth, as if he had a bulge of tobacco, and turned to his horse. Enrique kept chewing his jerky and fixed a gaze on the coral cloud on the eastern horizon.

"This is the day," he said. "The day I've dreamed about for so long."

Dutton tightened the cinch on his saddle. "Don't start drawin' blood yet, *amigo*. Getting to El Paso is one thing. Finding Valdar is another."

Dutton scolded Pang for jumping in the saddle before checking the cinch. The Chinaman climbed back down and Dutton checked it for him.

"How long do you think it will take us to find him?" Enrique said.

"Depends. We hit the saloons and start asking questions. We may get into some scuffles, and we need to try our best to stay out of jail. I've been thinking that it might be best to talk to the sheriff first. Then again, he may be on Valdar's payroll and botch the whole thing for us."

"How do you tell?"

"I can usually read it in people. It's not too hard. It's the friendly people I don't trust. The wolf in sheep's clothing, if you know what I mean."

"I do," Enrique said, standing, then brushing his hands together.

The three men mounted and rode, and a mile later they kicked their horses to a trot. An hour later they came to some rough, scrubby terrain near the end of a mountain pass. They slowed the horses. Horned toads sunbathed on the rocks, and lizards of many sizes and colors darted into cover.

Another hour passed and they came to a flat, covered with the same sand and scrubby brush that decorated the valleys, only now it looked like an endless sea. Dutton stopped his horse, and the other two rode up on either side of him.

"Another hour," he said. "El Paso is almost due east at the end of the flat."

Enrique stared in that direction and took a deep breath.

Pang held the reins up closer to his chest. "I say we make the horses run. Cut the hour in half."

Dutton shook his head. "*Amigo*, these horses need water. We punch their ribs any more than we have been and they won't last a mile. If we keep our pace, we'll be in El Paso close to nightfall. We all know that Valdar is more active at night, so there's no hurry. If he's already in Mexico, then we need a new plan anyway."

Neither of the other men argued with the sheriff, and he drew a nod from each of them. He led them into the flat, riding slow, heat bearing down on them like a stove, seeing nothing but sand and scrub, but with each step of their horses they smelled the sweet scent of blood.

When they came within view of the Rio Grande, the horses smelled the water and moved a little quicker. El Paso and Ciudad Juárez came into sight as well, with many wooden and adobe buildings, and before long they could see people roaming about and smell the smoke and cinder of urban life.

They let the horses drink to relief then led them along the river. A Mexican woman sat on her knees on a sandbar not far down the shore and dipped a piece of clothing into the river then scrubbed it on a rock. Before long she saw them and stopped her work and watched them cross.

Enrique looked back for signs of Sereno, but was sure he was far from town. He stayed away from cities. Just as in the days when he and Father Gaeta traveled to Tucson, Sereno would stay on the outskirts and surface again somewhere on the trail.

After they crossed the ford, they mounted their horses and rode into a street. Anxiety loomed throughout Enrique as the reality of where he was set in like an anticipated storm. The street was dusty, and dust made a film on everything around them. At times dust devils whirled and a tumbleweed made its way across the street and lodged against a building. Often they'd pass a hitching rack and a water trough, and it required a little effort to keep their horses from venturing off course to take a drink.

They passed a saloon, less like the *taberna* in Hachita and more like the one in Tucson; wood-sided with pane windows and a batwing door. Dutton made a steady acknowledgment of the place, but kept on riding. Eventually they came to a cross street and Dutton stopped. He looked in both directions, right then left, then kept his gaze on the left and turned his horse in that direction. For a while they rode dead center down the street, passing very few pedestrians or other riders, and then Dutton merged to the right and stopped at another hitching rack. That's when Enrique noticed the iron bars on the windows.

Dutton dismounted and tied his horse. "Pang, you're pretty good at keeping a watch on things. Enrique and I will go in and have us a chat with the sheriff here. We shouldn't be long."

Pang stepped down and held on to the reins of his horse while Enrique tied his and followed Dutton inside. When they got inside, they saw the badged lawman standing, looking out the window and sipping a cup of coffee. His head was hatless but creased where a hat had been, and his hair was dark, parted, and slick with oil. When he turned to look at them, his eyes were gray but gentle and the skin around them creased like spiderwebs. He sported a thick brown mustache that covered his lips and dripped coffee, which he licked off before drying the 'stache with a finger and thumb.

Dutton nodded a greeting.

The lawman nodded back then looked back outside. "Why is it," he said, "that whenever I see a Chinaman I sense trouble?"

Enrique wondered about Dutton's impression of the man, and whether or not he thought the lawman would help them.

The lawman turned and set his coffee cup on a desk, then sat in a chair behind it. He put his elbows on his desk, rubbed his eyes, then exhaled loudly. "It's Valdar, isn't it?"

Dutton and Enrique exchanged glances.

"That's right," Dutton said. "We've tracked him here. Do you know where we might find him?"

The lawman pinched his lips and looked out the window again. "You know, I took this job to protect the good citizens of El Paso. But I've had a problem doing that, mostly because of the riffraff that blows in here like grains of desert sand. I was lured here after a spell as a lawman up in Indian territory. I had no idea what I was getting into, and the ones that lured me here knew exactly what I was going to face. But one thing they knew about me was that I was hardheaded and honest. They knew I wouldn't quit if it killed me."

"I'm a lawman like yourself," Dutton said. "From Tucson. My posse deserted me."

"I'm sure I know why. Valdar's a hard character. As bad as I've ever known. But if you think I'm going to just tell you where to find him and let you go off on your own, you're mistaken."

"I'm willing to compromise, Sheriff."

"If I knew, we'd already be after him. It ain't just me and fellers like you. There's an army major and a regiment over at Fort Bliss that wants Valdar's hide, as well as a Texas Ranger outfit camped by the river. Hell they got a thousand-dollar reward out for him, and bounty hunters around here are thicker than January molasses. I'm quite sure none of them are aware Valdar is around or you'd see Rangers and uniformed men all over this town trying to weed him out."

Dutton looked at the floor, thinking. "Valdar surely knows there's that much of a price on his head."

"You bet he does. He's got *amigos* like roaches all over this town. There's no telling who you can trust and who you can't. I think he even enjoys the chase."

"Then that will make him hard to find," Enrique said. "If the army comes out, then it will be much harder."

"You make a good point," the lawman said. He looked at Dutton. "I'd give a year's pay to get rid of that evil son of a bitch and get things back to normal around here."

Dutton sat in a chair in front of the desk, took his hat off, and hung it on his knee. Enrique stood by the door.

"Give us the night," Dutton said. "Let us find out where he is, then we'll come to you and you can alert Fort Bliss and the Ranger party. Maybe we can surround him, smoke him out, and gun him down."

The lawman seemed to ponder the idea.

Enrique stepped close to the desk and slammed a fist on its top. "Like hell!"

Both men were startled by his reaction.

"I did not ride this far and spend half of my life waiting to kill this man to have him gunned down by the army. His blood is mine!"

Dutton combed a hand through his hair and sighed. "*Amigo*, I respect your feelings, but you ought to know by now that Valdar is not one to tangle with alone. You've been close enough to see the evil in his eyes. You ought to be thankful that we've got the support here that we have. For your family's sake, let's put an end to this man."

Enrique glared at Dutton, then at the lawman, and turned and walked out, slamming the door behind him. Pang stood between the horses, anxiously awaiting his report, but Enrique only paced the planked walk, back and forth, cursing and biting his upper lip.

"What is it?" Pang said.

Enrique stopped pacing and glared at him. "Tell me, could you live the rest of your life knowing someone else killed Valdar rather than you with your own hands?"

Pang wrinkled his brow. "I'd never really thought of it any other way."

"Me neither."

"But he is one man, and you and I both want his blood. Who is to say which one of us gets the glory?"

Enrique chewed on the Chinaman's words. He'd never really thought of it either. But he supposed now that so long as he had a role in it, and it was either him or Pang who killed Valdar, he could live with it. But he'd be damned if he would stand idle while they waited for the army to fire their bullets into the Demon Warrior.

The door opened and Dutton stepped out, his hat donned. He only looked at Enrique for a short moment then went to his horse.

"Where are we going?" Enrique said.

Dutton mounted his horse and pointed a chin to the east. "There's a place yonder that the sheriff said is a hangout for friends of Valdar. I thought we'd pay a visit."

Enrique didn't have to think about it and quickly mounted his horse. Pang followed, and Dutton turned to them both.

"I'm not going to tell either of you what to do, but I'm warning you to stay calm and keep your wits about you."

"Have I failed you yet, Sheriff?" Enrique said.

"Don't worry about me," he said. "Just be careful not to fail yourself."

They turned off the street and down an alley that took them out of the direct sunlight, shaded as it was by two-story buildings on each side. Halfway to the sunny end of the alley, they came to a nook and a back entrance. Dutton stopped and dismounted and the others followed.

"What is this place?" Enrique said.

"My understanding is it's a private back-room saloon frequented only by the roughest of characters. In other words, friends of Valdar."

They tied their horses and Dutton pulled out each of his revolvers and checked the cylinder. Once satisfied, he cracked his knuckles and motioned to the door. "Let me do the talking, and follow my lead."

"Do you want me to stay with the horses?" Pang said.

"No, not this time," Dutton said. "We're likely to need you more inside."

"What if Valdar is in there?" Enrique said. "A Chinaman will stand out, and he will certainly recognize us."

Dutton exhaled. "You're right. Regardless, if there's trouble, Pang won't know it unless he's inside. Pang, keep your hat brim down low. You're dressed like a Mexican, and it's likely dark enough in there that no one will know unless they see your face."

Pang nodded.

"All right, boys," Dutton said. "God be with us."


The room was dark, as they'd expected. It smelled of perfume and sweat and smoke from cigars. It was a small room, not much bigger than the *taberna* at Hachita, but with a door in each wall led to another room. In the first room there was a solitary table with an oil lamp on it and four empty chairs around it. The lamp was lit but still shed very little light on the windowless room.

Though the room was empty, they could hear voices and the laughing of women. They walked forward and peeked into the other room, and there were several men sitting on stuffed chairs while women in corsets gave them liquor to drink and bare skin to touch. They found a table against the wall and sat down. Enrique acknowledged a stairway in the far corner of the room and a short balcony above.

A woman came to them. She was young, with long brown hair and brown eyes, but not a Mexican. Enrique saw something familiar in her eyes, but thought little of it.

"This is a private place. You do not belong here." Her voice was hollow and coarse, without emotion.

Dutton pulled out his leather pouch of silver and tossed four coins on the table. "Whiskey if you got it. Preferably the Tennessee or Kentucky kind."

The young woman looked at the coins cautiously. "I see that it is not only whiskey that you want."

"Bring the bottle," Dutton said. "And tell your boss we have business."

She swiped up the coins. Enrique kept looking at her face. She returned a few minutes later with a bottle and three shot glasses. She poured for them. Dutton was quick to slug his whiskey down, but Pang hesitated. Enrique leaned forward to have a better look at the young woman.

"I've seen you somewhere before," he said.

The young woman looked at him closely and studied him for a moment, then poured Dutton another shot. "No, I would remember. I do not know you."

Enrique brought up his glass and drank half of the whiskey in it. He stretched his mouth then closed his eyes and drank the rest. The woman tried to pour him another, but he grabbed her wrist. Whiskey slopped out of the bottle and onto the table. She looked at his hand, then directly at him.

"Are you sure, *señorita*?" he said.

"I do not know you." She jerked her arm from his grasp and walked away.

Enrique thought long and hard about her. He was sure of his intuition, but he could not place her. The only location he likely could have seen her was Tucson. It was the only place where he'd seen other people, especially a woman like this. Very few strangers ever wandered into the mission.

Especially women, or beautiful women for that matter. But there was something different about her. And it was in her eyes that he had seen it.

They watched her walk up the stairs and to a door by the balcony. She knocked and a wedge of light appeared for a moment, then a man appeared at the rail. His face was dark and leathery, clean-shaven but sun-worn like a dried apple. He looked over the rail at them, shook his head, spoke something to the woman, then went back into the room and closed the door. She walked back down the stairs, holding up her cotton skirt as she stepped. This was the first time Enrique had seen her from this point of view. Though she was attractive, she was not done up and she looked tired and overworked.

She walked back to their table and looked directly at Dutton. "My *patrón* says he does not know you and wishes you to have your drink and leave."

She turned to walk away, but Dutton stopped her.

"Tell your *patrón* that we have three young girls with golden hair at our camp and we're looking for a buyer."

Enrique was surprised at Dutton's boldness.

The woman looked at Dutton silently for a moment, then back at Enrique. "You do not look like the type. You look more like bounty hunters, or maybe Rangers. I must ask you to leave now."

She walked away and left the room through a swinging door that led to a kitchen. A minute later she walked back in and tended to her business as if nothing had ever happened. Then men appeared in the same doorway—three altogether, young men, all Mexican, with guns holstered at their sides and one with a shotgun in his hands. They spread out across the room.

"Oh, here we go," Dutton said.

A realization suddenly hit Enrique. *"Dios mío!"* He stood from his chair and turned toward the woman.

"Hang on there, pardner," Dutton said. "We can't just go head-to-head with these *hombres*."

Enrique walked toward the woman. Dutton and Pang shared their confusion, then followed him immediately, and the man closest to the bar moved in. Enrique stopped, grabbed the woman's arm, and turned her toward him. She looked at him with scared eyes.

*"Tengo hambre,"* he said.

She looked perplexed. "This is not a *restaurante, señor.*"

They stared at each other silently, and the more he looked at her, the more sure he was.

"But only you know what I like. Remember, Amelia? *Huevos con pimientas—*"

Her jaw dropped then quivered, and her eyes studied him and welled with tears.

A shotgun blast went off. Enrique grabbed his sister and pushed her to the floor. Across the room the entertaining women screamed, and along with their customers they dove for cover.

Dutton picked up a chair and threw it at one of the armed men. It gave the sheriff just enough time to run and tackle the man, wrestle him, and knock him out cold. Pang somersaulted then dodged another man, kicking the shotgun before he could shoot. He then punched the man's stomach and flipped him over his head to crash onto a table. The third man came running and aimed his pistol at Pang. Enrique threw his knife, and it stuck directly in the Mexican's chest. He groaned and grimaced, shot his pistol aimlessly, then fell to the floor.

All the commotion brought the man upstairs out of his room. He drew a pistol and shot three quick rounds. Pang dove to the floor for cover, but Dutton growled and grabbed at his abdomen.

"Sheriff!" Enrique yelled. A deafening shotgun blast rang out from behind him, and the man on the balcony dropped his pistol then fell headfirst over the rail and down onto the tables near Pang below. Enrique looked behind him to find Amelia holding a smoking shotgun.

He looked at her, her face gleaming and wet from tears. She looked at Enrique, dropped the gun, and sobbed. He embraced her. "Amelia!"

He held her tight as she cried. But it was not for long, as she looked up into his eyes then held his face with both hands. *"Mi hermano. Por fin, mi hermano."*

"I am in disbelief," he said. "I have long dreamed of this day."

She smiled lightly, her dark eyes very wet with tears. "I, too, have dreamed of this day. Just look at you. You have grown into a man." Then her face grew solemn. "But it is not safe for you here. You must go."

He grabbed both of her arms. "I am not leaving without you."

"You have to, Enrique. He will kill you!"

He gripped her arms tighter, clenched his teeth. "I have waited my life to find you, Amelia. It was my life's will to do so. If I were to leave here without you, I would rather die. So risk my life to save you I will."

Pang shouted across the room. "The sheriff has been shot!"

Enrique and Amelia ran to him. Dutton lay on his back,

grimacing, his face sweating and his shirt soaked with blood.

Enrique kneeled at his side. "Is it bad, Sheriff?"

"One grazed my arm," he said. "Then another went in and out my side. I'll be okay if we can stop the bleeding."

"He must have a doctor," Amelia said. "I will show you, but we have to get out of here quickly. My *patrón* has many friends."

They all agreed and helped wrap Dutton's wounds with makeshift bandages that Amelia made from bar towels. Enrique and Pang each held a side of Dutton and helped him walk out the door and into the alley. They stayed in the alley and walked a block away to a back door, where Amelia knocked. There was no answer, so she knocked again, several times and louder.

"I'm coming!" said a voice on the other side. The door opened, and a bald, gray-bearded man wearing glasses and a black vest looked out at them. He looked at Dutton and down at the blood and told them to bring him in.

The doctor had them put him on a wooden examining table. Dutton grimaced while the doctor removed the bandages. Blood ran down the table and dripped onto the floor.

"Ah, you did well," he said. "Just enough pressure to keep the bleeding down. Don't look like anything important was hit. I'll get you sewed up and rebandaged, then hope for the best."

"What are you saying, doc?" Dutton said.

"I'm saying that you'll heal up so long as we avoid infection. As of now that's your only danger."

"Well let's make it quick. We've got a job to do."

"I'm afraid that's out of the question. You'll need at least a month of inactivity. Maybe more. You need healing time, mister."

Enrique looked solemnly at Pang.

"Now," the doctor said, looking at all of them, "leave me alone to attend to your friend. You can all wait in the parlor."

They walked out slowly and followed the doctor's instructions. He closed a curtain between the rooms, and they all sat on wooden chairs padded with red center-tucked velvet.

Enrique looked at Amelia. "Can you help us?"

"All I can tell you is to leave town. If I go with you, they will track me down and we will all die. So go and spare your lives while you still have them."

"You know I cannot do that. *Mamá* and *Papá*, they are dead. Valdar's men killed them. Did you know this?"

Amelia stared gravely. "No, I have always wondered, but I did not know."

"Have you been here all of this time, in El Paso?"

"*Sí*," she said. "Most of the women he captures go to Mexico. But he kept me for his own."

The thought of it made Enrique regret he hadn't come to El Paso sooner.

"My *patrón*, the man I killed, he and all of his men look after me while Valdar is away. I always dread the day he returns. About a year after he brought me here, I finally gave in to him. Before that, every time he came to me I fought him. After a while I realized it was what he liked, so I stopped doing it, figuring he'd take me away and sell me somewhere else. But it did not work that way. He just didn't come around as often, and I remained here, his prisoner, his mistress, his slave." She looked at Enrique and smiled. "I kept my mind at peace only because of hope." She knelt in front of him and held his hands. "Hope that one day my family would come for me. And at last that day has come."

He rubbed a hand along her cheek. "Yes, it has."

"That was a horrible day, when they came. How did you get away from them?"

"Valdar and his renegades . . . they would have killed me, too, but I escaped. I lived in the wilderness for days. I thought a lot of our grandfather, and coming here to find him."

Amelia looked sadly away. "I thought of that, too. Occasionally, strangers would come, and I would ask them if they'd heard of him, but nobody had. I always hoped that one day someone would, and that he'd come for me. But I'm not sure even our grandfather could have withstood the power and influence of Valdar."

"Like you, I still hope to find him. The priest told me to have faith, because with the right amount of faith, all things are possible."

"The priest?"

"Father Gaeta. He took me in shortly after Valdar's visit. I stayed with him at the mission all these years."

Amelia smiled. "*Mamá* would have liked that."

"I owe much to him," Enrique said. "More than I'll likely ever repay."

"And he approves of this? You taking vengeance?"

"He is letting me make my own choices."

"I am afraid for you, Enrique. Do you have any idea how bad these men are?"

"Did I not see the bodies of *Mamá* and *Papá*? I saw more than I ever care to see again. It is what drives me. I believe it is my destiny. I have already killed Beshkah. Now there are two left."

Amelia seemed astonished. "*You* killed Beshkah?"

"*Sí*. I was glad to do it."

Amelia stared solemnly at the floor. "Beshkah—dead."

Pang leaned forward, holding his hat between his knees and fondling the brim. "Valdar is coming back here, and he has my fiancée."

Amelia looked up at both of them.

"That's right," Enrique said. "It is not only me and my own yearning. Pang has his as well, and together we will see justice done."

Amelia rose to her feet and looked out a window as the setting sun cast many shadows on the street. "There is a place not far from here, by the river, an old mine. When he comes to town with women, he hides them there until he is ready to cross the river into Mexico. I should know. I spent a month there many years ago."

"Can you tell us how to get there?" Enrique said.

"No, but I can take you there."

"No, Amelia," Enrique said. "It's too dangerous. Stay here with Dutton and the doctor, and we will come back for you."

She turned to him. "You are forgetting, *mi hermano*, that I am your *big* sister. I have endured much since I was taken from you and brought here. My heart is hard but my mind is clear. There is nothing I am afraid of now."

Enrique acknowledged her willfulness. "All right. But what if we rescue Sai Min? After that, where do we find Valdar?"

"Finding Valdar is never hard," she said. "It's knowing who to ask, and then finding the courage to face him."

Pang took a deep breath, his nostrils flared. "We're half-way there, then. You supply the knowledge, we'll supply the courage."

The doctor sewed up Dutton and bandaged the wounds, and the new trio moved him to a hotel room and put him to bed. The doctor agreed to check on him hourly. The loss of blood made him weak, and sleep found him easily.

Amelia stayed with him while Enrique and Pang went back for their horses. It was dark now, and they knew they'd be able to sneak into the alley without being spotted. But when they got there, their horses were gone. They retreated back to the hotel, and Amelia told them that she was sure the horses were taken to the personal livery of Francisco Juarez, her late *patrón*. She also told them that it was there that Valdar kept his own horses that he brought Juarez to sell.

"Horses he stole, you mean?" Enrique said.

"*Sí*," she said.

"It could be that the horses and mules he took from us on the trail are there as well."

"But we should not be greedy," Pang said.

"There will be a young livery boy there," Amelia said. "He will not be difficult for me to persuade."

"Very well," Enrique said. "Let's go get our horses back."

The livery was near the center of El Paso and almost a stone's throw from Fort Bliss. While approaching the livery, they could hear the sound of a fiddle playing inside the fort and see the shadows of guards near the corners of the bastion. Amelia went inside through the main entrance of the livery, while Enrique and Pang snuck in on either side, through the corral and into the stables. As she had envisioned, the young Mexican stable boy was there, and she found him carrying a wooden pail of water. He seemed startled by her presence and slopped the water as he stopped.

"Pedro," she said. *"Necesito los tres caballos de los gringos. Dónde están ellos?"*

Pedro dropped the bucket and ran. Two men appeared out of the darkness of the stables. Amelia recognized them as men who worked for her *patrón*. She took two steps backward, and then Pang swung in from a rafter above and lit on the ground in front of them. The men stood frozen for a moment, then one of them smiled, one front tooth missing, and lunged at Pang. The Chinaman darted to one side, and the man fell clumsily into the straw and dusty muck of the stable floor. The other man rushed Pang, but Pang blocked his punch with a forearm, jabbed his chest, and as the man fell, wheezing, Pang knocked him unconscious with a jab to the back of his neck. The other man rose from the ground, his face partially covered with dust, making his lips appear pinker than they really were. Straw fell from his hair and his eyes glared as if they were equipped with their own weapons.

He growled and dove for Pang, but Pang jumped, twirled on one foot, and brought the other foot up against the Mexican's chin. He spit blood through his lips and his eyes rolled back in his head before he hit the ground. Slowly, he tried to get up, but Pang delivered the same crippling move to the back of his neck that had put his *compadre* out of commission.

Enrique made his presence known, holding a pitchfork. Pang turned to see who he was, then stood at ease. Once Enrique saw the two men down, he leaned the pitchfork against a stall.

"Glad I could be of help," Enrique said.

Pang wrinkled his mouth and shook his head.

Amelia came forward and kneeled down by the men, then looked back up at Pang. "I've never seen a man fight like that. You have some gift."

"A gift taught by my father," Pang said. "A good and wise man." His face grew solemn. "A man whom Valdar murdered in cold blood."

Amelia did not know what to say, but she now understood his purpose more than before.

Enrique put a hand on his shoulder. "Let's get our horses and go find Sai Min. Then, we can pay our respects to Valdar."


The young Mexican ran with all his might to the adobe hideout south of El Paso. He saw a faint light and stopped to catch his breath, then took off again toward the sounds of laughing and drinking men and women.

When he came to the door, he knocked wildly. All grew silent inside, and then he heard pistols cocking. The door opened slightly, and the eye of a woman peeked out at him; then she turned and said: "*Es el chico del establo.*"

The door opened, and Baliador looked out at him, his eyes glassy and red. "*Qué quieres?*"

Pedro caught his breath before he spoke. "*Los gringos— ellos tomaron—los caballos.*"

Baliador pointed toward the darkness with his chin. *"Largo de aquí."*

Amelia led the way to the abandoned mine. They rode hard and fast, knowing the boy ran scared and would likely be alerting Valdar of their coming, and that possibly, as a precaution, he would remove his female captives before they arrived. What battered her mind the most, though, was how she had betrayed Valdar to the point that she could never go back, and that he would kill her for sure if she did. Her confidence in leaving with her long-lost brother increased after seeing him throw the knife, but mostly after he mentioned killing Beshkah. That would have been no easy feat for anyone. Her faith was sealed after seeing Pang fight, and knowing that they both had powerful skills as well as motives to see Valdar's blood. Their abilities and their reason were all that was needed to succeed, and likely the best chance Amelia would ever have to get out.

Enrique was amazed at how well Amelia rode, and how sound her thinking was after having been through such a long, horrible period with Valdar. He had tried to prepare for the day he would find her, and after talking to the priest about it, he'd become convinced that if she was still alive, her mind likely would be gone. It was a true miracle that she had been able to keep hope alive, and it was a powerful witness to her inner strength.

They rode the horses to a lather, through a bitter darkness that enhanced the jittery feelings among them. Enrique worried some about Pang's inept riding talents, but one thing about being a drag rider in a rush was that all one really had to do was hang on. That, it seemed, Pang could do well.

They followed Amelia down into a ravine and wound around several knolls and into a dry streambed, which no doubt helped feed the Rio Grande somewhere along the way. She slowed and eventually came to a halt and dismounted. Though it was hard to see, there was the faint outline of a hillside. Suddenly a match was lit and Amelia's face was cast in a dark orange. She found a lantern and lit it, then held it down by her feet.

"Fresh tracks," she said.

Enrique got down from his horse and looked at them with her. "Soft prints," he said. "Not heeled shoes. Valdar wears moccasins and leggings from the Apache."

"But there is only one set of prints," she said. "And they go in, but don't come out."

"*Sí,*" Enrique said, knowing what she meant.

Pang looked down at the prints as well, and then down into the shaft entrance. "Is this the only way in or out?"

"That I know of," Amelia said. "But I am not sure."

Amelia and Enrique looked at each other, as they knew what Pang was getting at. If there was no other way out, then Valdar and Sai Min were still in the shaft. Either way, they knew they had to go in.

Enrique held the lantern and led the way. Amelia held on to him by the tail of his serape, and Pang followed close. They all ducked from the low clearance.

"How far in?" Enrique whispered.

"I'm not sure," Amelia said. "It's been a long time. But he chained me to a wood beam. That I do remember."

Enrique thought of the damp darkness, night or day, that anyone would have to endure in this place, and that his own sister had been held captive here in her youth so many years ago. The strength in her, to be here now, amazed him.

They continued walking and came to a dead end, a rocky mass as if the tunnel had collapsed.

Enrique sniffed the air. "This is fresh. I smell fresh earth."

"Then there must be another way out," Pang said. "And he blocked us from finding it."

Enrique thought for a moment, and looked behind him. "And it could be a trap, one that he is setting for us."

"But why?" Pang said. "Valdar is not afraid of anything. Why leave us in here? Why would he be afraid to confront us?"

"I think I know," Amelia said.

"What is it?" Enrique said.

"Valdar may be a hard, evil man, but he is very superstitious. You said you escaped him before?"

"*Sí*," Enrique said.

"Not many, if any, ever have. Believe it or not, he is afraid of your medicine. Something he learned from the Apache. He is afraid that if you've done it once, then you will do it again, and that he must take the woman away before you can get to her."

"Which means," Enrique said, looking back down the dark tunnel of the shaft, "trapping us in here and holding us up would be a good plan for him."

They immediately turned and ran, the lantern nearly

flickering out with ever step and stride. Then they heard the explosion; the ground shook and a cloud of dust came rapidly toward them. They fell to the ground and covered their faces. Enrique lay over his sister to protect her. After several minutes, when the dust had settled more around them, they uncovered their faces, trying not to choke on the dust that remained. It was still too thick to see more than four feet beyond the lantern.

"What do we do now?" Pang said.

"We dig ourselves out," Enrique said.

"What if he's waiting on the other side to ambush us?" Pang said.

"He will not wait," Amelia said. "He will be taking your fiancée to Mexico as fast as he can."

"Then we have no time to waste," Enrique said, crawling up the pile, grabbing a rock at the top, and tossing it down. Pang helped him dig. They pulled rocks away until their fingers and knuckles were bloody and they had enough of a hole to crawl through. Pang held the lantern, and Enrique went first, on his stomach, then Amelia; then Pang passed the lantern through and crawled through himself. The hole was tight, and the sharp rocks cut into them as they crawled. Pang tumbled down to the other side, and like a pack of coyotes they ran free into the night.

# BLOOD FOR
# JUSTICE

They looked around cautiously, still fearing ambush, but taking note of Amelia's notion of what Valdar might be doing. So far she had been right. The only problem they could see now was that, once again, their horses were gone.

"He stole them once, why not again?" Enrique said.

"We still have a chance," Amelia said.

"What are you saying?" Enrique said.

"The trip into Mexico is not one he will take without many men, horses, and supplies. He has not had time to prepare for that. It is likely that Baliador will gather all his men and gear and meet him at the Socorro ford."

Enrique thought for a moment. "Can you tell us how to get there?"

"No, but I will show you."

Amelia started to lead them, but he grabbed her arms.

"No. It is too dangerous. I have lost you once. I cannot bear to do it again."

She glared at him and jerked her arms away. "I did not endure all these years to only hear of Valdar's death. If you are to kill him, I will be there to spit in his dying eyes."

Enrique was caught by her words and could not hold her back. She turned and led them down the dry bed, walking and stumbling for several hours in the darkness. The new day started to break, and a purple haze formed over the desert around them.

"How much longer?" Pang said.

They all stopped, and Amelia raised her head and pointed. "Just over that rise. We must approach it carefully."

Enrique looked at Pang, and Pang looked back at him. Enrique knew that the Chinaman was feeling the same way. This likely was it. The showdown that they all had anticipated since the beginning of their journey. They knew, too, that if Valdar wasn't there, then he had made his way into Mexico and it would be a long and difficult journey to stay after him. Regardless, they would do it. It didn't matter to what land, how long, or how far the Demon Warrior went, they would follow. They would find him and kill him. His blood would be the payment for all he had done to so many, and there was no time limit on collecting it.

The sky was bright now and the morning haze was dissipating, but the birds let everyone around them know that it was a new day, that another day of survival had begun.

The trio found a spot on the final bend of the streambed where they could lie and peer over into the Rio Grande.

Enrique scanned the terrain, but he saw nothing. He was afraid they were too late.

"Are you sure this is where he crosses?"

"*Sí*," Amelia said.

Enrique studied the far side of the riverbank looking for telltale signs of tracks where several horses might have crossed. But he saw nothing.

"How many men will he take with him?" Enrique asked Amelia.

"Usually about ten. They are men who work for Juarez. All Mexicans and good with guns. They know Mexico and Mexico knows them."

"If that many men have crossed into Mexico, they didn't do it here."

"They have not crossed yet." Amelia stared across the river, her eyes cold and almost lifeless. "I can smell him."

Enrique looked across the river, then back at his sister. He grabbed her arm. "Amelia, what are you saying?"

"He is over there . . . by those cottonwoods."

Enrique looked across the river at the tall, twin cottonwoods that stood majestically over the southwest bank. The roots of one bared themselves on the bank of the river. The other was almost hidden behind it. But he saw nothing else but the trees, and smelled nothing either. "Are you sure, Amelia?"

"Pang's fiancée is tied to a rope between the two trees. Valdar, he is sleeping, waiting for his men to arrive. I should know. I went on that journey once, but ended up coming back with him."

Enrique looked at Pang and pulled his knife from its sheath. "Well then, how about we interrupt his *siesta*?"

Enrique raised his head and peered toward El Paso, and saw no other riders. Once satisfied, he crawled down the bank and the others followed. They waded into the water and moved very slowly to make little noise. The water was no more than knee deep, but it weighed heavy against Enrique's feet. It felt like one of those dreams he'd had as a child, where he was hunting and saw a prize elk, but his arms would not move to lift his bow, or his bow seemed too heavy to lift, and the game just stood there taunting his inability to make the kill. It was not so much the memory of the dream that consumed Enrique now, but the anticipation of what lay beneath the cottonwoods. The thought began to boil inside him—the memory of all that had happened to his parents and to Amelia, and all the nightmares and time alone before he went to the mission. It stirred an anger that made him gnash his teeth and form his free hand into a fist. He gripped his knife until his hand turned white and his fingers throbbed. Now he sensed Valdar's presence, too, and he believed his sister. Valdar was there, and his time had come.

Pang waded through the water close behind Amelia. They all made slow, short strides. There was a point where the water came almost to their waists, between the sandbars of the ford, but they kept moving, the power of the reckoning fueling them forward. Pang thought about how quickly his life had changed, and looking at Enrique in front of him, he knew, too, that if not for him, and Sheriff Dutton, he would likely not have gotten this far. It was destiny, and it would not fail him. The thought of it made him feel larger than life itself and stronger than he'd ever felt. Not even the water that surrounded his legs could restrain him from claiming his revenge and bringing justice to his family.

Halfway across the river Enrique stopped, as if he'd turned to stone. His head turned slowly, and then Pang heard them, too. Horses clopped and snorted. He turned and saw them approaching the bank of the river behind them. At least a dozen riders, all Mexican, wearing wide sombreros. When the riders saw them, they fanned out along the bank, and then four riders rode into the river, two on each side of the trio. The horses' feet splashed wildly. They stopped a good thirty yards away and peered directly at the the three of them thigh deep in the muddy Rio Grande.

Pang looked up at the center rider, whom he immediately identified. It was Baliador, and he smiled at them, then put his fingers in his teeth and whistled.

Valdar appeared from behind the southwest bank. He looked down on them and studied the situation from every angle. At first he did not smile, but seemed very concerned as his head moved about, but at last came the devilish grin that they'd all come to know so well.

At least they knew now that Amelia was right. But the harsh reality of the sudden predicament did not take long to set in.

"Ah, *mis amigos*!" Valdar yelled. "How far you have come. I take it I have something you want?" He lifted up Sai Min by her arm. Her face was badly soiled, her hair in disarray, and her eyes bulged as she called out Pang's name. She now wore a dirty white cotton dress.

Pang knew there was nothing he could do. He clenched his fists and looked all around him, trying to make a plan.

Valdar laughed and pointed a chin at Baliador, who rode down the bank and into the water. He grabbed a rope from his saddle, twirled a loop, and tossed it around Amelia. A quick pull and a spurring of his horse took her under the water, and Enrique dove in after her. Baliador pulled quickly, but Enrique found the rope and brought his knife up to cut it. The rope snapped and curled like a snake across the top of the water. Enrique rose with Amelia in his arms, both of them coughing out water and breathing hard.

Angry, Baliador jumped from his horse into the water and high-stepped toward them. Pang jumped into his path, took a deep breath, and remembered a teaching from his father, from a lake back in China. He could almost hear the voice of his father and his teaching.

"No matter where you are, my son," Hingon said, "your body can find balance. Focus all the power to the part of your body that is free."

Pang took another deep breath, raised his hands above his head, and put them together, as if his arms were a roof over him. Baliador stopped and snarled and pulled a revolver from his holster. Pang dove into the water, and he could hear the muffled gunshots and bullets whiz by him, but he found Baliador's legs, wrapped his arms around them, and with all his strength pulled him under. The renegade was strong, but because he had fallen backward, most of his energy was being used trying to recover and get back to his feet. Pang took advantage of the moment, let go of his legs, and put all his body weight on top of Baliador. He grabbed his neck with both hands and pushed down. The renegade's arms swung up and beat frantically on the Chinaman's sides and back. Pang held on, holding his breath under the water but hoping that Baliador couldn't hold on, that he would give in and suck water into his lungs.

* * *

It seemed that the desert fell silent around them. Not a bird chirped. There was not even a breeze to make a leaf flutter or to echo off the eroded shoreline. They all watched in this silence, to see who would rise from the water in triumph. Enrique's stomach turned when he saw that the first to rise was Baliador, his eyes wide, but suddenly he bobbed back down, lifeless, his body floating and turning in the current. Then Pang rose, all the way to his feet and gasping for air. He breathed hard, water running from his hair and onto his face and dripping from his chin and arms. He glared all around with his eyes wide, and then he arched his arms to his sides, clenched his fists, looked up in the sky, and yelled. It was not a typical cry of triumph, but definitely one of victory. A release of all the torment he had left, as an offering to his father's spirit.

It did not take long for Valdar and his men to respond. Guns rose on each of the mounted horsemen, and as they aimed, Enrique dove for the water, pulling Amelia in with him. He could hear the dull piercing of bullets hitting the water all around him. He held his breath, feeling his sister's hands grab hold of his waist, then her arms wrap around him as they tumbled underneath the shallow river.

Before long he could not take any more and needed air. He rose to face the wrath of Valdar and his men. Now it was all a stand of faith.

As Enrique rose from the water, he felt Amelia's hands release him. The gunfire suddenly stopped, and he gasped for air as his head surfaced. He made way to his feet, looking all around him as he stood, dripping wet. All the men on horseback had lowered their rifles. Valdar came closer to the river and was looking on with anticipation.

Enrique found Pang lying in the water, somewhat bent over and grimacing.

"You okay?"

"My leg is hit, but I am okay."

Enrique looked around him, wondering why the mounted men had stopped. He looked to his side, and to his horror found the body of Amelia floating facedown.

"No!"

He dove for her, turned her, and found her limp and lifeless. Then he saw the bloodstain grow over her chest where a bullet had penetrated. After all this, she had led them to Valdar only to meet her death. How could it be? He wanted to hold her, but just as he thought he had no more hatred for Valdar, it rose within him to a level that made him feel as towering as the cottonwoods that stood high above them all.

He let go of Amelia and looked at Valdar. He breathed in and out, clenched his fists and gnashed his teeth, and yelled from the bottom of his wet lungs. "NO!"

He lifted his legs high from the water and marched toward the shore. Valdar glared at him, back-stepped, and fell down. He jumped back up, drew his pistol, and aimed it at Enrique. Bullets flew all around him, but Enrique remained steadfast toward his enemy. Valdar emptied the gun and after two dead clicks growled and tossed it into the water. He turned to run up the bank, but a sudden rumble stopped them all. Valdar turned and looked opposite him, but Enrique wouldn't stop his pursuit. The rumble increased, and there were gunshots all around. Enrique expected a bullet to penetrate his back and knock him into the water, but then he saw the Mexican riders crossing the river and none of them shooting. The rumbling continued to grow, and two of the riders were shot off their horses.

Puzzled, Enrique turned. Several riders appeared all around him, charging into the water, shooting rifles and handguns. They were mostly blue-coated soldiers, some in civilian clothing, dusters, cotton shirts. Nearly a hundred of them.

After all of the Mexican riders had been shot or had given in, several soldiers rode up to the southwest side, and in a matter of seconds they had surrounded the entire area.

Valdar stared in defeat. He pulled a knife and started after Enrique, but before he made a second step, he arched his back and grimaced. He stared, ghostly, for a moment, then fell forward, a hatchet stuck in his back. On the bank above him stood a lone figure, and once Enrique realized who it was, his mind and body locked in astonishment.

Sereno walked down the bank toward Valdar. The Demon Warrior squirmed and tried to crawl, but he stopped when Sereno turned in front of him. Valdar turned to his side and looked up at the young Tohono O'odham, who spat in his eye. Valdar snarled and reached for him, calling out a loud blood-curdling cry.

Guns fired all around him and Valdar's body was riddled with bullets. His body jerked and rolled as bullet after bullet annihilated his entire body. Fragments of his skull, flesh, and bone littered the river bank and the water.

It happened so fast that Enrique had no time to react. Sereno? Of course, it all made sense now. Father Gaeta said he had found him with his family slaughtered and his throat cut. It was Valdar who had done it, and Sereno was more afraid of him than anything else. He must have known of Enrique's pursuit and been bound to go along with him. He had, and like the rest of them, he had found his justice.

It all made Enrique realize just how little control he had over anything, including, sometimes, himself. He had killed Beshkah, with his own arrow. Pang had killed Baliador with his own hands. Sereno, along with many men, better than a hundred nameless soldiers, men that represented all the people, had done their duty in claiming revenge for the many lives ever affected by Valdar.

A soldier released Sai Min, and she ran down the bank and into the water. She cried and wrapped her arms around Pang, then helped him out of the river. He limped along the shore then fell to one knee, and two soldiers climbed down to his aid.

Six other riders rode down into the river; only these weren't soldiers. One Enrique recognized immediately, not only by his smiling eyes but also by the white sling that held his arm. Riding alongside Dutton were five men in big hats and with badges on their chests. Then he recognized the lawman from El Paso. The others he assumed were deputies.

He turned and took hold of Amelia's body and dragged her to the shore. He sat down and laid her head in his lap, then bent over her, kissed her forehead, and wept.

Dutton slowly stepped down from his horse, grimacing from the pain in his side. He kneeled beside Enrique and put a hand on his shoulder.

"I'm so sorry, *amigo*."

Enrique rubbed his hand over Amelia's forehead, then

leaned over and kissed her again. "She was so close to freedom. So close."

"Oh, she's free," Dutton said. "A freedom that we all will know someday. A freedom from this earth and all the hell that goes with it."

Enrique looked up at him. "I had so much I wanted to share with her."

"You gave her everything. And she knew that. Be grateful that you were able to have this time together. It's more than a lot of other families got."

Enrique gave Amelia one last kiss, and two soldiers came and carried off her body.

All the badged lawmen had dismounted and gathered around Enrique. They walked to Valdar's body, blood-soaked and almost unidentifiable. Sereno sat down next to Enrique. A single tear ran down his cheek as he stared at the Demon Warrior's body.

Enrique shook his head. "I am amazed at how I feel. I'm happy to finally see Valdar dead, to see justice served for so many, yet I feel deep sorrow for my sister."

Dutton nodded. "I reckon the Good Lord doesn't want us to take much glory in the killin' of others, regardless of how bad they are—He wants us to realize killin' for what it is and how much it costs."

Enrique looked at him.

Dutton looked down at Valdar's body and bit his bottom lip. "Yeah, it never ceases to amaze me how death, no matter who it comes to, is never pretty."

"The doctor said you were to stay in bed," Enrique said.

"Yeah, well, I knew what you were doing and I had to alert the law."

"I should be mad at you, but for some reason I am not."

Dutton nodded. "Well, I'm glad of that. Hopefully someday you'll understand my thinking. To you, tracking and killing Valdar was personal. To me, it was professional. The way I look at it, together we got the job done. Now maybe people in this region of the earth can sleep a little easier at night."

A buckboard drove up and stopped, and Enrique watched the soldiers lift Amelia's body into the bed of the wagon and cover it with a blanket. "*Sí*," he said with a sigh. "Father Gaeta will be pleased."

The three men, along with Sai Min, gathered by Amelia's grave at the cemetery near Fort Bliss. A priest came out to read over the body and then left them alone. The grave digger waited for them to walk away, then commenced to doing his job of filling the grave.

Pang limped from the bullet wound in his thigh, and Sai Min held his elbow to help him along. As they continued on, three riders came toward them. They wore large hats and long dusters. On the lapel of each duster was a shiny badge.

"Who are these men?" Enrique said.

"I reckon we're about to find out," Dutton said.

The riders came to a halt and dismounted. All removed their hats and offered condolences. The one in the center spoke first. He was the tallest and oldest of the three. His mustache was gray and his face swarthy and aged. His hair around his ears was gray as well, but the crown was still dark. When he returned his hat to his head, it seemed to cover and protect what youth he had left.

"Name's Tom Crawford. We're all Texas Rangers."

"What can we do for you boys?" Dutton said.

"Well, it's more like what we can do for you. We've been over at the fort, listening to the whole story about what happened with Valdar." The ranger half-smiled at Enrique and Pang. "My compliments on a job well done. You've brought down enemy number one, and the good people of Texas aim to pay you well for it. We've deposited fifteen hundred dollars in reward money at the Bank of El Paso. There was a a thousand dollars on Valdar's head and five hundred dollars each on Baliador and Beshkah."

Dutton wrinkled his brow. "My figuring brings that to two thousand dollars."

The Ranger nodded. "I believe the story that you killed Beshkah, but the law requires a body, dead or alive, in order to collect a reward."

"That's okay," Enrique said. "I don't want it anyway. And I doubt Sereno would want it."

The Ranger pinched his lips and raised his eyebrows. "Well, your choice, I reckon. And how you divide it is up to you. There's fifteen hundred dollars there with each of your names on it. You can draw it out at any time. We appreciate your good work. Now we best be riding on." The Ranger tipped his hat and nodded at them, then turned to leave.

They watched the Rangers ride away, and Enrique tried not to feel angry. Though he knew $1500 was a decent sum of money, he saw no value in it relative to the lives of his family. After so many years, enduring all that he had, witnessing all the horrors and suffering all the pain, to be given $1500 from the government for doing a good deed was like a slur on his *mamá*, *papá*, and Amelia, as if the government had spat on their graves. He couldn't help but think of what Dutton had told him, about working a trade and using cash money to purchase items for living. It might be the way of the times, but it certainly wasn't Enrique's way.

# DESTINY'S
# TRAIL

They recovered all their horses at the livery, as well as the two mules and the pack donkey. They would be able to give Benjamin back his horses, which pleased Enrique.

Since the livery had fallen under new ownership, with a manager appointed by a judge, they kept all their animals there until Dutton and Pang were both in better shape to travel. Pang's wound, luckily, was just a graze on the thigh, but deep enough that the soreness made walking difficult. As with Dutton, the doctor insisted on patience, rest, and healing time to avoid bleeding and infection.

They went to the bank together, and Enrique was surprised that Dutton refused to take part in the reward. With $1,500 lying on the counter, the sheriff just held up his hands. "No, boys, I was on duty. I was already paid to do this, and it would be unethical for me to accept anything.

Besides, you three lost family and endured years of pain over this. All I did was take a risk, and that's part of my job."

Enrique looked down at the three stacks of paper notes. They were intimidating and foreign to him. He looked back at the sheriff. "Will you at least carry the money for us and protect it until we decide what to do with it?"

Dutton offered a slight grin and nodded. "It would be my pleasure."

The sheriff took the money and put it in a saddlebag, and they all left the bank and walked Sai Min down to the stage office. Pang accepted some of the money and purchased Sai Min a stagecoach ticket back to Tucson. He wired her father to let him know she was coming. Three days later, he said his good-bye, and that he would see her again soon, when he returned with Mun Lo. Though he worried about sending Sai Min alone, after all this time apart, he was convinced a stage-coach ride was much safer than a ride through the wilderness.

What surprised Enrique and Dutton most, however, was the conversation that took place before she boarded the stage.

"Are you sure you'll be okay?" Pang said.

She looked at him tenderly. "It is the right decision. You have a new life now. The money you gave me will go a long way in China. You will be a hero to them."

Pang kissed her hand and helped her onto the stage. Apparently they had talked, and she wasn't the only one to notice a difference in Pang. Some saw it as a hardness, but Enrique understood it more than anyone. It was the light of destiny in his eyes, a new sense of freedom and an under-standing that his purpose was other than what he'd planned.

He knew he would never be content being married and running a business in Tucson. It was better for Sai Min to go back to the Mother Country and find a better husband. He was sure that he could sell the business to one of his Chinese elders, but then what would he do? Just as in the pursuit of Valdar, he would let the moments of time and the circumstances of the days help him decide.

While Pang and Dutton rested, Enrique would stroll through town. He visited Fort Bliss and shared his story with the soldiers there, and one night they had a dinner in his honor. One of the officers took note of Enrique mentioning his grandfather. The officer pulled him aside later that evening and told him he remembered his grandfather and his grandfather's brother. He said that his brother was very ill and owed a large amount of money to an *oficial* in Hermosillo. The last the officer had heard, the brother had passed away and Enrique's grandfather had agreed to absorb the debt with his servitude.

This was the first time since burying his sister that he had had any indication of what he might do next. He knew he would have to go back to Tucson with Pang and Dutton, if anything to help ensure that Mun Lo made it back safely. And he would check back with Father Gaeta. After that, he wasn't sure, yet, like Pang, he knew that day-by-day living would lead him down his next path.

Hermosillo, he thought. Servitude? He wondered how much the debt was. With this in mind, he talked himself into it and told Dutton he would need his $500 after all.

On his way down a busy street, he noticed several men unloading freight from a buckboard. He couldn't help but notice what was in one of the large crates, and he stopped to ask about it.

"Excuse me, *señor*," he said to a stocky man supervising the workers. "Where is that going?"

"Not sure now," he said. "It was ordered by a congregation, but someone skipped town with their entire collection. I'll likely have to take a loss on it just to get rid of it."

"How much for it, right now?"

The man narrowed his eyes and scratched his chin. "Young man, if you'd be so willin', I'd take twenty dollars cash money right now. I'll even have these fine young men load it for you."

Enrique unfolded his money and the man watched him eagerly. He paid the man twenty dollars, and the man shook his hand happily. "You saved me a lot of heartache, young man. Now, where can we load you up?"

"That would be my next question, *señor*. Where might I purchase a buckboard and harness?"

The man pointed. "Down yonder a ways, you'll see a corral and a blacksmith. Right next to it is a feller that can fix you right up."

Enrique smiled and shook the man's hand. "*Gracias, señor*. I will return shortly to be loaded."

Within two hours Enrique had purchased a buckboard and harness and had retrieved his mules from the livery, hitched them up, and had the freighter load his new purchase.

Within a week Dutton and Pang were ready to travel, and both seemed delighted that they had a wagon to carry the supplies. They were all surprised that Sereno joined them and rode in the back.

Dutton made mention that because of the wagon they'd have to take a slightly different trail, and he also wondered about the contents of the crate in the wagon.

"It's a gift," Enrique said.

Dutton nodded and didn't pursue it any further. It didn't matter about the wagon. They weren't in a time fix anymore. They could take their time and enjoy the scenery and the glory of staking their own claim on justice. Now it was definitely a time of peace, and a time to look toward a different horizon.

After seven days of traveling the stage trail of the lowlands, they arrived back at Benjamin's *rancho*. They were greeted by children and *vaqueros*, and before long the commotion drew Benjamin, his old lady servant, and Mun Lo from the *casa rancho*. What surprised them most was to see Mun Lo in a Mexican dress, her long black hair flowing and exposed, with only her eyes and skin tone to give away her true ethnicity.

She smiled and ran to Pang and hugged him.

He looked at her, up and down, and apologized. "When we get back to Tucson, we will get you proper attire."

She looked down embarrassedly and then glanced at Benjamin. Benjamin grinned and came to Pang offering a vigorous handshake. The Chinaman could tell something was up, but he didn't quite understand what it was.

The *vaqueros* took their horses and unhitched the mules, and they all went inside, where a large spread of food was prepared to soothe their hollow stomachs. They feasted on beef, peppers, tortillas, and wine, and each shared his own version of how the evil era of the Demon Warrior had been brought to an end. Benjamin raised his glass in a toast to the soul of his late fiancée. Then he looked at Mun Lo, who sat diagonally from him at the end of the table. He smiled at her and held her hand then sought out Pang.

"I think this is the best time as any to make an announcement," Benjamin said.

Pang and Enrique exchanged glances, acknowledging each other's confusion.

Benjamin stood, and looking toward Pang, he placed a hand over his heart.

"Pang, Mun Lo and I have come to an agreement. One that delights me, and I hope will delight you as well. With your blessing, I would like to make her my wife."

The room was abnormally quiet. All eyes looked at Pang, but he looked only at his sister, who sat quietly in her new apparel, with her head slightly bowed.

Benjamin continued. "I know this probably comes as a bit of a surprise—"

Pang rose quickly from his chair and stomped out of the room. He walked through the front door and out into the courtyard that was experiencing the dimness of the setting sun and the sounds of locusts in the trees.

Mun Lo had followed him. He stood in the middle of the courtyard looking up at the tops of the trees and into the dusky sky. She walked up behind him and put a hand on his shoulder. He turned around abruptly. A tear ran down his cheek.

"I'm sorry," she said, "if we've upset you."

He studied her for a moment. "This is what you want?"

"He is very good to me. The people here—they see me

as their own. There are all races of people and all are considered family. They would risk their own lives to protect another. I am at peace here, and I want to stay."

Pang grabbed both of her hands and held them firmly. "It is our custom for an arranged marriage. You know that. And since our father is gone, it is my duty."

"We are in a different land now. Customs here are different. If you love me, Pang, then you will want me to be happy."

A lump grew in his throat as he studied the sincerity in his sister's eyes. Oh, how he did love her. She was all that he had left. After all that had happened, he had thought long and hard about their destiny. Would it really come to *this*?

"It is my duty now to see that you are properly cared for," he said. "But I do not want to stay here with you."

She smiled. "You don't have to. You can trust that they will care for me."

"Do you think you can learn to love a white man, Mun Lo?"

"I already love him. We take long walks together, and ride on horses. He shares his dreams with me, and he is interested in my own. He is a kind and gentle man, who cares about all who live on his *rancho*. I've never been more at peace. I want to be his wife, and give him children."

By the contentedness in her smile, Pang could tell her feelings were genuine. After all that they had lost, how could he take this away from her?

"I can't help but think that Father would disagree with this," he said.

"But he is gone and you are in his place. I told Dick that I would not agree to his proposal without your blessing. He agreed, too, out of respect, that he would ask you first."

Pang looked at his feet, and then gazed around at the many buildings of the *rancho*. It was indeed a prosperous place, with many caring people. He thought of how well they had cared for the four of them after they'd nearly died in the desert. And he thought about life in Tucson. Truthfully, he knew of no other way he could provide such things for his sister. Times *were* changing, as were customs, and he would have to adapt like the rest. With this in mind, he looked at his sister and took a deep breath.

"I will agree on one condition," he said.

"What is that?"

"That before I go, I will see you married. That way I'll know it's done."

She smiled and jumped and wrapped her arms tightly around his neck. "He will be so pleased!"

He pulled her down and looked deeply into her eyes. "I can see that this is your destiny."

"I believe you are right."

He hugged her, and over her shoulder he looked off into the night. It seemed now that everyone knew what he or she needed to do, except him. It was almost exciting not to have an answer yet, but to know that something grand and fulfilling awaited him. It was more than enough, he supposed, to help him live with this decision and move on.

It was not a simple wedding. The women of the *rancho* decorated the adobe walls of the courtyard with blooms from the wild. There were yellow and white wildflowers, and a few violet and lavender. They placed the flowers in garlands of ivy and draped them along the walls. Mun's dress was white and made of silk, one that Benjamin's own mother had been married in. He'd kept it in a trunk for just this occasion. The women clipped a red rose from a bush that Benjamin had imported from the Midwest and planted in the courtyard. They tied the rose in her hair, which hung freely and without a headdress or a veil to cover her face. She came out of the *casa rancho* through the main door, and toward her brother, dressed in a borrowed suit from one of the younger *vaqueros*. He led her into the courtyard, over flower petals scattered by young girls, and to her groom, who was flanked by his foreman, the best man. A priest from a border mission had been brought in just for the occasion. He stood facing and centered to them all, dressed in a brown robe and holding a Bible.

The guests and witnesses, mostly family of the *vaqueros*, along with Enrique and Dutton, stood facing the bride as she entered. Pang offered Benjamin his sister's hand with a sincere nod, and after a reading of several verses by the priest, and an exchange of vows, the priest made his proclamation that they were man and wife. An announcement that was met with cheerful applause.

The feast afterward was an amazing outdoor spread, with long tables put together and covered in white linen, and numerous platters of chicken, beef, tomatoes, maize, *frijoles*, peppers, potatos, squash, tortillas, *pan*, apples, and pears. There were many pitchers of wine, and a *mariachi* performed with guitars, violin, trumpet, and vocals. Many danced, and the children all gathered around a *piñata*. It was a fiesta like none other, but what mattered most to Pang was how he saw his sister smile. It was a smile he knew he could live with.

* * *

Two days after the wedding, the trio rose early to head back to Tucson. It was not as difficult a good-bye as Enrique had expected. He half believed that Pang would not want to leave his sister, but the Chinaman did leave, and Enrique was proud of him for doing so. Even Enrique understood the challenges of the Chinese in Tucson, and Mun Lo would have none of those with Benjamin. It was a good thing for her to stay, and yes, he believed too, her destiny.

After two weeks of travel they arrived in Tucson. Dutton squared everything with the law, and after steady persuasion all charges were dismissed against Pang. To their surprise, Dutton also turned in his badge. The mayor and the judge tried to talk him out of it, but he'd made up his mind.

They rode with Pang into the Chinese district, where he found Vin Long seeing to the family tailor business. The old man greeted Pang joyfully. He informed him of Sai Min's safe arrival on the stage, and with the money Pang had sent, her father had agreed to send her back to China. She waited only a day, then was out on the next train that would take her to San Francisco.

Pang agreed it was best that she hadn't waited for him. "The first good-bye was hard enough," he said.

Vin Long fixed them all tea, rice, and soup, and listened to their stories. The elder listened intently, finally nodding after a moment of silence.

"It is as it should be," he said.

They all met outside Vin's home to say their good-byes. The sheriff bit his lip, removed his hat, and combed his hand through his hair. Pang stood with his arms crossed and peered down the alley at the canvas tents of his Chinese neighbors. Enrique stood next to the buckboard, prepared to climb into the seat. Sereno sat on his knees in the buckboard, peering over at them.

Enrique could tell it was an uneasy moment for all of them. He extended his hand to the sheriff. The sheriff received it and shook it firmly.

"I'm not sure how we could have made it without you, *señor*," Enrique said. "You showed us the way, and I learned a lot from you."

"I learned a lot from you, too, *amigo*."

"From me?"

"From both of you. You taught me a lot about spirit and faith. Things I'd forgotten about, or maybe I never really understood."

Enrique nodded. "Now that you've resigned as sheriff, what are your plans?"

"I thought a lot about that on the ride back here. I decided to go back to Missouri to see my brother. I may stay, and I may not. I just want to see some old country and old kin."

Enrique and Pang both shook his hand again.

"Safe travels, *amigo*," Enrique said. "I will say a prayer for you."

Dutton smirked. "Just pray for the railroad. Hopefully that's what will get me there."

They all laughed while Dutton mounted his horse. He looked back toward them, touched his hat brim, then rode away.

It was one of those happy-sad moments again. They watched him ride until he disappeared down a side street, knowing that would likely be the very last time they'd ever see Sheriff Chas Dutton. A man too good for a corrupt law, and Enrique believed that he, too, was now at peace with himself and the world.

He turned to Pang immediately, knowing that this good-bye would be the hardest.

"I will not forget you, my friend," Pang said.

Enrique nodded. "You have a brother in me. I will always be here for you."

"What will you do now?"

"Go back to the mission, visit with Father Gaeta for a while, and when the time is right I will ride to Hermosillo. My grandfather is my only family. I must try to find him."

Pang nodded and looked at the ground.

Enrique sensed a lonesome feeling. "What about you? Have you thought about what you will do?"

"That's all I think about, but I have no answer yet." He looked down the alley again, then back at Enrique. "I have some unfinished business here. Vin Long has agreed to buy my father's tailor business."

"You are selling? How will you make a living?"

"I don't know. I want to try to bring my mother here. I have the money to do it now. But for me, I've thought about just traveling. What money I have will get me by a long while. You and the sheriff have taught me how to travel. I want to see the earth."

Enrique pointed a chin south. "Should you want to accompany me to Mexico, you're welcome to come along."

Pang nodded. "I will give it serious thought."

Enrique thought about shaking his hand, but he knew it wasn't enough. He reached out his arms and embraced the Chinaman. Pang was slow to return the embrace, but he did so firmly.

Enrique held back any emotion that tried to well up within him, let go of his friend, then turned and climbed up on the buckboard. Without looking back, he snapped the reins and guided the mules toward the Santa Cruz, silently praying that he would one day see his Chinese brother again.

It was good to be in familiar country again. The Santa Cruz and the land and wildlife around it had been Enrique's home all his life. He knew every bend from the mission to Tucson, every rock that protruded from the river's banks, and every stream that delivered its water. He knew the birds and animals that drank from it, and he was sure, too, that they knew him. But life along the Santa Cruz did seem different, even though it probably wasn't. He supposed it was because now Valdar was dead that the fear was gone, and the dread of the past resolved. It was good, for a change, to be anxious to be back home, rather than anxious to leave, always wanting to go away for revenge and to seek justice. They were feelings that were all gone, and life had a new direction.

Father Gaeta was in the garden working when Enrique came into view of the mission. When the priest noticed the wagon, he held the hoe at his side and removed his straw hat, wiping the sweat from his forehead with the sleeve of his robe. Enrique wondered if the priest recognized him driving a buckboard, and realized that he did when he dropped the hoe, donned his hat, and raised both arms.

"Enrique, my son!" he yelled.

Enrique stopped the mule team in front of the mission. The priest came to greet him, scattering chickens that were pecking the ground in the yard. Enrique stepped down from the wagon, and the priest smiled widely and then embraced him.

He let go but held Enrique at the biceps with both hands. "I'm so glad you're back safe. That was most important to me."

"It's good to be back."

The priest looked over the mules and the wagon, and then noticed the brown-eyed boy in the back.

"Sereno?"

The priest looked up at Enrique, his mouth open.

"It's a long story," Enrique said.

The priest reached in and touched the boy on top of the head and smiled, then noticed the crate. He leaned over the rails. "What do we have here?"

"It's a present—for you."

Enrique jumped up into the back of the wagon and with the blade of his knife pried open the crate lid, then pounded down one of the sides.

The priest's eyes rounded when the contents became exposed. "Gracious Father!"

Enrique smiled. "You said the mission never had a bell. Well now it does."

"But Enrique, how could you afford such a thing?"

"Reward money, for helping subdue Valdar."

The priest's eyes were now more relaxed and his face solemn. "So, you accomplished what you set out to do?"

"As good."

"I see. Well then, I do believe that justice was served."

Enrique nodded. "Yes, it was."

The priest slapped his shoulder. "And now you're back home. And Sereno! I bet you're both hungry. Let's get something to eat."

They walked into the mission, and Enrique enjoyed the meal of soup and bread, and the conversation, which was the same physical and mental sustenance that had made him into the man he had become. It was a nice change, too, to have Sereno eating with them, instead of in the stable, by himself. He couldn't talk, of course, but he listened well, smiled occassionaly, and was truly at peace.

The priest had become a father to both, and Enrique loved him as much. When he shared the story of how he found Amelia, the priest understood his joy, and also his added grief. But just as Dutton had said, the priest reminded him that he should be glad for what little time he did have with her. The wisdom. Always the wisdom.

Enrique also shared with the priest his intentions for the future. He did aim to make the mission his home, a place to come back to, but he wanted to help people. He decided to spend some time with the priest, help with the harvest, then go to Mexico to look for his grandfather. He thought, too, that before he went south, he would go back north and visit Pang, and hopefully persuade him to come along. Foremost, he liked how they worked together, and he believed that together they could help other people seek out justice when they'd been wronged. It was something they were good at, and something that was worthwhile doing.

The priest wasn't that receptive to the idea, but he did commend Enrique on his big heart. "It is good that you want to help people," he said. "I just hope that violence is not always to be your way."

"I learned from Pang, Father, that protecting oneself is a right. So long as we do not seek violence, our defense is a method to avoid it."

The priest nodded. "You can see it that way if you want, Enrique. It is your choice, and your right to exercise your own free will. Just remember the lesson of turning the other cheek. And that there will always be consequences to face when you choose not to."

"I do remember those lessons, Father. You taught me well."

"And remember those are God's lessons, not mine."

"Yes, Father."

Not long after their meal Enrique went back to his room, unpacked his things, and came across the skin of the rattlesnake he'd killed the day he found Pang in the desert. He smiled and thought how nice it would be to make a wallet of the skin and go to Tucson someday and present it to Pang as a gift. Yes, he would do it.

The next day the priest fixed a rope and pulley, and he and Enrique muscled the new bell into the tower. After three hours of sweat and toil, they hung it on the wooden beam. Enrique had never seen the priest smile the way he did at that moment. He could tell it was a smile of true joy.

The priest put his arm around Enrique and together they admired the bell.

"It is a very fine gift, Enrique. I am forever grateful of your thoughtfulness."

"Aren't you going to ring it?"

"Well of course!"

The priest grabbed the rope tied to the bell yoke and gave it a tug. It was a sound that the Santa Cruz had longed to hear for many generations, and which had now come to life. It was a sound that the priest would make every day at high noon, on holidays, and on other occasions during the harvest, or during baptisms. He was not certain who would hear it, but it was mostly symbolic, and like everything else related to the priest's work, it was an exercise of faith.

To Enrique, the bell became something different than just a tool for the religious trade. Whenever he was off down the river, out hunting, or on his favorite bluff looking out over the desert, and he heard the priest ring the bell, it represented the end of era. It was a special sound for all the Sonora to hear. The sound of freedom, possibly, but foremost to Enrique, it was the sound of justice.

# ABOUT THE AUTHOR

Steven Law comes from a family of storytellers that inspired him with both folklore and the written word, all of which derived from sources from their pioneer days to the novels of Mark Twain and Laura Ingalls Wilder. During college Steven felt inspired to write his first novel, which a constantly busy schedule forced him to put on hold. After receiving a bachelor's degree in business administration, Steven spent several years in corporate America, and he also nearly completed a master's degree in business education. Increasingly disenchanted with his career and course work, he dropped out of graduate school to devote his life to writing. While struggling to make a name for himself, Steven worked as a community newspaper reporter, a columnist, and a freelance Web publicist for writers and writing organizations. For more than fourteen years he has worked with several acclaimed authors, such as Pulitzer Prize finalist S. C. Gwynne, *New York Times* bestseller Stephen Harrigan; *New York Times* columnist Peter Applebome; award-winning novelist, singer, and songwriter Mike Blakely; and the late Elmer Kelton.

## ABOUT THE AUTHOR

Now a successful novelist, Steven lives in the Missouri Ozarks with his son, Tegan, two cats named Pepper and Sylvester, and a shih tzu named Obi-Wan Kenobi. *El Paso Way* is his fourth novel.

Visit his website at www.stevenlaw.com.

# Don't miss the best Westerns from Berkley

. . . . . . . . . . . . . . . . . . . . . . . . . . .

**LYLE BRANDT**

**PETER BRANDVOLD**

**JACK BALLAS**

**J. LEE BUTTS**

**JORY SHERMAN**

**DUSTY RICHARDS**

. . . . . . . . . . . . . . . . . . . . . . . . . . .

**penguin.com**

M10G0610

**Penguin Group (USA) Online**

*What will you be reading tomorrow?*

Patricia Cornwell, Nora Roberts, Catherine Coulter,
Ken Follett, John Sandford, Clive Cussler,
Tom Clancy, Laurell K. Hamilton, Charlaine Harris,
J. R. Ward, W.E.B. Griffin, William Gibson,
Robin Cook, Brian Jacques, Stephen King,
Dean Koontz, Eric Jerome Dickey, Terry McMillan,
Sue Monk Kidd, Amy Tan, Jayne Ann Krentz,
Daniel Silva, Kate Jacobs...

You'll find them all at
**penguin.com**

*Read excerpts and newsletters,
find tour schedules and reading group guides,
and enter contests.*

Subscribe to Penguin Group (USA) newsletters
and get an exclusive inside look
at exciting new titles and the authors you love
long before everyone else does.

**PENGUIN GROUP (USA)**
penguin.com

M224G0